Harry Scores a Hat Trick

WITH PAWNS, PUCKS, AND SCOLIOSIS

by Mary Mahony

Illustrated by Catherine M. Larkin

Happy Reading!
Mary Mahony

Redding Press • Belmont, MA

Susan A. Pasternack, Editor

Illustrations © Catherine M. Larkin

Cover and interior design © TLC Graphics, www.tlcgraphics.com

Portrait on page 151 © Joe Demb Photography, 59 Louise Rd., Belmont, MA 02478

Printed by Bang Printing, Brainerd, MN

Fiction

RL: 4–6

Library of Congress Control Number: 2003095938

ISBN 0-9658879-3-6

Dedication

This book is dedicated to the many athletes who experience the disappointment of a medical condition that abruptly affects their ability to continue with a sport or the heartbreak of an injury after a great deal of training and hard work. Some of you are only derailed temporarily and once healed are able to get back on track. In other cases, the medical condition or injury is permanent and demands that you let go of a dream that you once held so tightly. Whether it is someone competing in the National Hockey League, for an Olympic medal, or on a local level like Harry, the disappointment is nevertheless very deeply felt. On all of these playing fields you are great role models, just like Harry. Each one of you has shown that you have other strengths that go beyond your impressive athletic abilities. I personally thank each of you for giving one more amazing triumph for us to remember.

If you have experienced a chronic medical condition or an injury, I hope you will be able to return to your sport in the very near future. But for those of you who cannot, I hope the characters in this story will open your minds and your hearts to explore strengths that you may not even know you have. Life is not always fair, but it is good, and I hope each of you will learn to focus not on the unfair part of life, but on the good. For that wonderful show of strength and determination that you have shared, I sincerely thank you.

A special thanks
to the following people:

Carroll Blake	Nan Braucher
Thelma Burns	Darius Cohen
Emily Cook	Allison Guillory
John Hall, M.D.	Isiah Haynes
Dan Kelleher	Maureen Martin
Rodney Moody	Adrianne Slattery
Moira Slattery	Elli Stern
Ben Weissman	Cedric White
Karen White	Kyle White

Edward "Poppy" Burns

Marc Asher, M.D., University Distinguished Professor, University of Kansas Medical Center, Kansas City, Kansas

Tom Brownscombe, Chess Master, former Scholastic Director of the U.S. Chess Federation

Tamara L. Dever and Erin E. Stark of TLC Graphics, for their wonderful book design

Catherine M. Larkin, for her outstanding illustrations

A special note of thanks to my editor, Susan Pasternack, for adopting each of my books as her own. Her insights and suggestions make my books a far better read.

Introduction

H i. I'm Harry Jones and this is the sequel to the first book about me called *Stand Tall, Harry.* Before you read Chapter One, I want to give you a little background about what went on before. I live in Boston and I'm part of the METCO program. METCO stands for the Metropolitan Council for Educational Opportunity. That is a very long way of saying that I am bused from my house in Boston to a school way, way out in the country. I used to think this was a really big deal, but I've met a lot of other kids who have chosen to go to schools that are far from where they live. I finally realize that it's okay not to go to your neighborhood school, but I also need to tell you that it sure has its challenges. I am one of only about eight African-American students in my school. Very few of my classmates really know that an urban environment has lots of great things to do. I hate it when kids start talking about all the bad stuff that happens in the city, because I haven't seen any bad stuff. Anyway, things can happen just as easily in the country, too.

I guess I should also go back and tell you a little bit about my life. I have one half-sister, whom I really consider to be my whole sister, and her name is Consuela. She lives down in Georgia, where she goes to college. My favorite sport is hockey, but I hit the boards in my first big game last year and got injured so I couldn't play for the rest of the season. When I was in the hospital for my injury, they told me I also had scoliosis, which they explained is curvature of the spine. Did I need to know all that on top of the injury? Right before I got hurt, I had made this new friend at my school named Jack. Jack and I liked to play chess, so he brought me a magnetic chessboard as a gift when I got hurt. After a while, we got into chess so seriously that we signed up to play in a tournament. I thought it was awesome, but Jack got real nervous so he stopped going to tournaments after that. I continued and then one day another one of my friends, Tommy, suggested to Jack and me that we start a chess club at our school. So we did. We called it the Mercier Movers since our elementary school was called Mercier and you move your pieces on the chessboard. Get it? Mercier Movers!

I played in chess tournaments almost every weekend last year and that's where I met another chess player, named Dawn. She and I became very good friends. In fact, she taught me a lot about chess and about lots of other things, including scoliosis. It was the scoliosis that made Dawn have to wear a back brace. But even with the back brace, Dawn could do just about anything she wanted. She was very cool and also very nice.

After playing in several chess tournaments, I got so good that I was invited to play in the Kings of K–12 Chess Tournament out in Colorado. The Kings of K–12 Chess Tournament is by invitation only and it is a very big deal. If you win that tournament, you get invited to some of the national tournaments. My dad and my Grampy came with me to Colorado and then the biggest surprise of all was that my mother, my sister, and my friend Jack also got to see me play. How cool is that?

Dawn was invited to play, too. She had played a lot longer than I had and this was just one of many tournaments she had joined. But this was the biggie! We were both really very nervous about the possibility of competing against each other. It was a very cool tournament and also a very hard one. If you want to know more about it, you can read *Stand Tall, Harry*. Oh, yeah, one more thing. You might wonder why the book is called *Stand Tall, Harry*. Well, because my Grampy, who knows everything that is important to know, says that people always need to stand tall and be proud of who they are. Now, if you go to Chapter One, you can find out who won the Kings of K–12. Also you need to know that a hat trick is when you score three goals in one hockey game. My hat trick consists of three things, but believe me, they aren't all hockey goals!

Happy Reading!

Harry Jones

Chapter One

Having my whole family and my best friend with me in Colorado was hard for me to believe. My parents and my Grampy looked like they were about to cry every time I looked at them. It's a good thing I had Jack and Consuela there. At least they were excited in a normal way. Dawn had warned me it would be like this, and boy was she ever right.

After I gave everybody the grand tour of the tournament area and introduced them to the people who had organized it all, we went up to our rooms. Dawn and her parents were in the elevator and of course we almost went past our floor. Parents just never seem to stop talkin'. As we were getting off the elevator, my dad asked Dawn and her family if they wanted to join us for dinner. At first I wasn't sure that was a good idea since we'd be opponents in less than twenty-four hours, but nobody remembered to ask me. Dawn's family accepted immediately and, as I looked over at Dawn, I had the feeling she was thinking the same thing I was: What a weird dinner this was going to be.

Back in the room we did a little reorganizing. Grampy and Consuela went to their rooms, and Jack and I got to share a room. It was really neat to be almost across the country with your best friend.

We had a few places to choose from for dinner. Dawn and I got to decide so we chose the restaurant that had live singers entertaining you while you eat. Our parents were pretty surprised at this, but finally they all agreed.

When we entered the restaurant, a lady came right over and introduced herself as Carol, the hostess, and told us she would seat us in just a few minutes. Dawn and I noticed that the salt-and-pepper shakers on the tables looked like chess pieces. In fact, they had made the whole place look like part of the tournament and it was pretty neat.

They sat us down at a table right near the stage and Grampy was so excited about our seats that I don't think he even remembered we were there to eat. When the waiter gave us our menus, we saw that many of the meals had chess pieces in their names: the appetizers were called Round 1 and dessert was the Last Round, which everyone seemed to laugh at except for Dawn and me. I ordered the Rook's Ribs, which I thought was pretty clever. I guess when they called themselves "Experts at Chess," they weren't kidding.

Our parents got along really well and, as it turned out, Dawn's father and my father had very similar jobs and got into this heavy computer talk about how these tournaments were run and how computers kept everyone in the loop. I thought it was the TV monitor that was doing all that, but I decided to keep quiet since this stuff was very complicated. I looked around the table, still not believing that we were in Denver, Colorado. It was just too awesome! For a second I caught Jack's eye and I could tell that he knew just what I was thinking.

"Harry, this is so amazing! Did you ever think our little chess games would get you all the way to Denver?" he said.

Before I could answer Jack, Dawn started to giggle and told us that when she got to her first really big tournament, she was thinking the very same thing.

Chapter One

Even though we were having a good time I could tell that Dawn was as tired as I was and I think we were each wondering when our parents would put their computers to sleep and pack it all in. When we finally said good night, no one mentioned a word about the tournament. But as I was walking away Dawn called out to me, "It's only a game, Harry, so don't worry about who wins. That's the first lesson in a big tournament like this."

When Jack and I got into our beds, we were quiet for a minute and then we both started to talk at the same time.

"You first, Harry. You're the chess champ so you get the floor," Jack said, half laughing.

"Jack, this is like some out-of-body experience in those science fiction books you're always telling me about," I answered. "Part of me is excited and part of me is scared about what's going to happen next. I go up and down like a bungee cord."

"Harry, you're going to win, I just know it," said Jack. "But let's say you don't win. Who cares? This has been so awesome and you'll still qualify for other tournaments. I heard Dawn's dad talking about more sponsors at dinner. This is big stuff, Harry, and it's just the beginning if you really like it as much as I think you do."

"Jack, what made you quit soccer?" I asked a little shyly.

"Whoa, Harry. Where did that come from? I thought we were talking about chess," Jack replied in a surprised voice.

"Come on, Jack. I don't want to talk about chess. It makes me too nervous about tomorrow's tournament. Let's talk about soccer instead."

"Well, Harry, I'll tell you if you promise never to tell anyone, not even your parents or your Grampy. Deal?"

"Sure, Jack. Deal, but this sounds really heavy," I answered.

Jack began. "I told my parents I didn't like soccer anymore, but actually I loved it. I had this coach my last season who was a screamer. No matter what we did on the field, he'd find something to scream about. His son was also on the team and he'd come up to me all the time and tell me not to make the same mistake I made at the last game. It was pretty bad, Harry, and after a while I felt like a soccer failure. I felt like I didn't belong out there. I felt like everyone was watching me make mistakes."

"But, Jack," I asked. "Why did you let the kid put you down like that? Why didn't you just tell him to back off and mind his own business?"

"Come on, Harry. It's not always that easy."

I was quiet for a minute and then answered, "You're right, Jack, but it's just not fair that some kid can bully you out of something you really love."

"Harry, you need to get some sleep. We'll talk about soccer another time."

I knew this was Jack's way of ending a talk that he was not feeling good about but I was glad that he had shared it with me. Jack didn't like to discuss stuff that bothered him. I kept thinking of ways to get Jack back into soccer. It sure beat worrying about a chess tournament!

I couldn't believe how well I had slept. Jack had to wake me up. I was kind of hoping that we wouldn't see Dawn and her family at breakfast. Last night was hard and I knew that seeing my opponent would give me the jitters.

Consuela came to the door while I was in the shower and visited with Jack. I could hear them from the bathroom laughing about something and I was kind of curious about what these two found so funny.

When I came out of the bathroom, both of them got real quiet so I knew they weren't going to share the joke and I was pretty sure it was about me. Before I got a chance to pump them, my parents and Grampy knocked on the door. This was for sure the "keep moving program" and there wasn't going to be much downtime, which was probably a good thing.

The restaurant was as packed for breakfast as it had been at dinner. I was really glad that Dawn and her family weren't there. I was feeling kind of uncomfortable about this last round. Not only was Dawn good, but she was my friend, and I knew that she would be having scoliosis surgery not long after the tournament ended. She had told me many times how important this was to her. Boy, it sure made me feel pretty awful that I might beat her.

Chapter One

After breakfast my dad asked me to go for a walk with him. I knew he wanted to talk.

"Harry, I have a feeling that this is not going to be very easy for you, playing the one person who has been the most supportive to you in all these different tournaments," Dad began. "Remember that when you get down to the final moves, you can't let yourself be distracted by how Dawn is going to feel if you win. If you let Dawn win that way, she won't feel that great about it. Do you understand what I'm trying to say to you, son?"

I really didn't want to talk about any of this, but I knew just what my dad was trying to tell me. I had played this tournament in my mind many times. A few of those times I had thought about letting Dawn win. The only thing worse than playing Dawn would be playing Jack or one of my other friends, like Hank or Herbie.

"I know you're just trying to help, Dad," I said, "but I don't want to talk about this right now because it's going to jinx the tournament. Can we just drop it and go back?"

"No problem, son. I think it's almost time for you to play," said my dad.

Chapter Two

When it was time for me to enter the room where Dawn and I and many other competitors would be playing our final round, I asked my family to let me go in without any big scenes. My mom insisted on a good-luck hug, Consuela and everyone else just gave me the old shoulder tap, and Jack showed me a thumbs-up. I was already feeling the pressure.

I glanced into the room and Dawn was already seated at the board. Her brace showed above the neck of her shirt and as soon as she realized that it was me looking in, she gave her usual nod and smile. The other kids I had met through Dawn also gave me a nod, and as I walked into the room I felt like I was with old friends. We kind of spoke our own language, the language of chess. These competitions took a lot of emotional energy because you had to be thinking every minute.

As I was getting into my chair and about to set up, Dawn started whispering something to me. I leaned over to hear her better.

"Harry, today you have to pretend that we aren't friends or else you won't play a good game. Let's promise that whoever wins, the other person will be really happy for them. Deal? Harry, just say deal 'cause we have to get started."

"Okay, deal, Dawn, but I just can't all of a sudden forget we're friends," I replied.

"Yes, you can, Harry, because I've done it many times before with other opponents. If I can do it, you can do it, too!"

Before I could answer, it was time to start the round. Dawn was playing the white pieces. Not only does white have an advantage, but Dawn was also the higher-rated player. I ended up with the black pieces, again.

I lost my concentration a few times and glanced over at Dawn. Her eyes never once left the chessboard, at least not that I could tell. Her concentration was amazing and I could see that she had meant it when she told me that I needed to pretend we weren't friends. She was totally connected to the game and nothing else.

Throughout the round I would catch myself about to make silly mistakes, but I corrected them just in time. I was tired, but I built up a strong opposition, almost feeling badly for Dawn. I started to wonder if she was almost too focused and distracting herself from the game. I know that may sound a little confusing but I hope you know what I mean. It's kind of like trying too hard.

When I started a mating attack, I knew that I had won. I glanced over at Dawn, who looked ready to cry. My right hand and fingers were absolutely frozen and I dreaded making the last move. It was as if I were playing chess in slow motion. I could feel Dawn's eyes looking at me as if to say, "Harry, what are you waiting for?" She seemed to be doing everything she had told me not to do.

Finally, I placed my fingers on my chess piece and made my move. I had won the tournament with a perfect score, 6–0. I didn't even want to look up at Dawn.

As I raised my eyes, Dawn's hand was right in my face.

"Congratulations. You did it. You're THE CHAMPION. Your family must be jumping up and down in the observation room. Harry, what's the matter with you? Harry, you won. You're THE CHAMPION!"

Chapter Two

"Dawn, I feel so bad. I wanted you to win, too," I told her.

"Harry, two people can't win. You know that. Don't feel bad. Feel excited. Harry, this is a really big deal. You won. Don't you get it? You won!" Dawn kept repeating it over and over again.

As I was escorted out of the room, a man was taking my picture and on the other side of him I could see Jack with both of his thumbs up and this big smile on his face. Out of the corner of my eye, I saw Dawn bury her head in her father's shoulder. As my dad walked past them, Dawn's father reached his hand out to congratulate my dad. Dawn looked up and gave my dad a big smile, telling him how happy she was for me, but I could tell that her eyes were watery.

They quickly escorted us away from the tournament room. Even though they had shut the doors, there was a lot of talking and rejoicing.

By the time I got to the rest of my family, it was slowly sinking in that I had won. Dawn and her dad followed us down and her mother was as excited for me as my own mother was, telling us what it was like when Dawn won her first big tournament. As I entered the room, I saw Consuela taking a picture of the wall chart that gave the final score. My family was so excited that the rest of the people in the room who were waiting for their own children to finish their rounds simply joined in the celebration. Grampy was as wound up as I had ever seen him and as soon as he started talking his eyes just filled up. I couldn't believe how emotional everyone was getting over a chess tournament. A reporter from the local Denver paper interviewed me and someone from a chess magazine was also asking me questions and taking pictures. Jack never left my side and even told the chess magazine lady that he was my best friend. Jack, who is usually pretty laid back, was as wound up as my Grampy.

Even though I was very happy, I was still thinking that Dawn had lost and would be headed home soon to have back surgery. As excited as I was, I couldn't get her loss off my mind. I found myself looking around the room to be sure that she was okay. Consuela seemed to be thinking about her, too, because after she finished taking pictures of the wall chart she went over and started talking to Dawn. Pretty soon I could see them laughing hysterically and I knew that Dawn was in good hands. For as long as I can remember, whenever I feel down, Consuela has always listened to me and our talks have always ended with both of us laughing. It was the thing that I missed the most when she went off to college. I really love having an older sister.

We had to wait for the rest of the players in the tournament to finish their rounds and then participate in the awards ceremony. It was kind of different standing up in front of a group of strangers. I was amazed at how excited everyone got for each champion. Some of the winners spoke two languages, English and one their parents brought with them from their homelands. They thanked the Kings of K–12 Chess Tournament organizers in both languages. That's one of the things I like the most about chess. You meet so many interesting people. All you really need is a chess set and a table.

After the awards ceremony we all had to rush upstairs and get ready to leave. I thought I would be sad about that because the whole trip was kind of like a dream. But I was excited to get home to Boston and to my school to tell everyone about the tournament so I didn't really mind going.

The sun had just begun to set behind the mountains when we were leaving our room. Just as my dad was about to do one last room check, I asked him if I could go back into the room I had slept in that first night. At first my dad thought there wasn't time, but then Grampy interrupted, "Oh, let the boy go in. He'll be quick. He must be looking for something."

I glanced over at Grampy and got the funniest feeling that he knew why I wanted to go into the room. I then grabbed the card from my dad, slid it into the slot, and waited for the green light to flash. I opened the door and quickly shut it behind me. I walked over to the window and looked up at the mountains just as the sun was about to hide behind them. I stood there for a moment thinking about my great-Grampy. My great-Grampy showed my Grampy how to play chess, my Grampy showed my dad how to play, and then my dad showed me. I guess you could call it a family tradition. I looked to the sky and whispered, " I hope you were watching, Great-Grampy. I won that tournament just for you. Thank you for being there with me because I just know you were watching. I just know you were."

I could hear my mother knocking on the door telling me to hurry up or we wouldn't make the plane. Jack asked if I had lost something as I started walking down the hall and before I could answer him my Grampy looked over and said, "I kind of think he found something. Something real special."

I slept on the airplane almost the whole way home. I was pretty excited to have Jack there with me, but we were both so tired that we hardly talked. Consuela took a different flight because she had to get back to school in Atlanta. Dawn and her parents were staying on in Denver for two weeks of vacation before her surgery since her school year had already ended. We had said our good-byes at the awards ceremony and our moms exchanged phone numbers so that we could go see Dawn back home after her operation. As we boarded I could see that even without Dawn and her parents, the plane was still full of chess players and their families, and unlike the trip out, it was a very quiet ride back. We were all exhausted and ready to move on.

Chapter Three

It was a lot cooler in Boston than in Denver. The pilot announced that the temperature was about 67 degrees and the sky was overcast. Poor guy can't just be a pilot; he has to be a weatherman, too. Everyone was kind of slow moving out of the plane. My dad said the time change would be hard for us to adjust to for the first few days. Even though I was wide-awake, it would be time to go to bed when we got home.

A lot of us still had our chess tournament shirts on. All kinds of people congratulated me. I was getting excited all over again and I couldn't wait to tell my friends about everything. I knew I was never going to be able to fall asleep. I already wished it was Monday.

When we got into the terminal, I could hear my friend Herbie yelling, "There he is, our buddy the chess king. Harry, Harry, we're over here!"

Herbie and Hank were standing there with these huge grins on their faces, making everyone look at us. The other kids from the tournament and their families were enjoying the show that Herbie was providing. Hank looked like he wanted to hide Herbie in a closet or stuff his mouth with something. Jack's parents were standing behind Hank and waving. It was a real scene and Grampy was lovin' every minute, making sure the rest of the people in the area knew what this was all about.

We spent what seemed like a long time talking to everyone and telling Jack's parents about how exciting it was to be in Denver and, on top of that, to win. I kept thanking them for letting Jack come. Herbie and Hank hung out with Jack while we got our luggage.

Getting everyone home was something else. Herbie and Hank had taken the subway to the airport and so Jack's mom and dad offered to get them home. Finally, we were heading out. I couldn't believe that my trip to Denver was over. It was a time that I knew I would never, ever forget.

When we finally pulled into our driveway, we were all pretty tired. We opened the door and I could hear the phone ringing. The answering machine had more messages than my parents had ever seen before. A lot of people already knew that I had won the tournament.

Tommy, my school friend who had formed the chess club with Jack and me, had left nine messages. Even my school principal, Mrs. Starck, and my fourth-grade teacher, Mrs. Lamont, had called. Then there was a message from a guy who's a chess Grandmaster, congratulating me on my incredible success. I think he's just a little bit older than Consuela, which is really impressive. Becoming a Grandmaster is a lot of hard work and skill. You earn your invitations to really famous tournaments and you have to win a lot of them to become a Grandmaster. Just having one of those special people leave a message on my phone was pretty amazing.

Sunday night turned out to be one of the wildest nights of my life. The only time that ever came close was the night before Consuela went off to college. Even after I got myself into bed, I could hear the phone ringing and ringing, and my mother was just talkin' up a storm. Even my dad got on our other phone and then I could hear both of them, sometimes at the same time. My dad normally hates the phone so this was pretty crazy stuff.

For me, the best part of all was when my Grampy came in to say good night to me. He couldn't even get the words out, his eyes got all watery, and he hugged me so hard I almost stopped breathing. As he walked out of my room, he turned around, looked over at me, and said, "You sure know how to stand tall, Harry. You sure know how." I had never seen him so emotional.

As he was leaving my room I called out, "Grampy, you taught me how to stand tall, remember? You showed me the way, Grampy."

How would you like to wake up, totally exhausted, with your mother standing over you saying, "Rise and shine, chess

Chapter Three

king, it's time to get ready for school." I had been hoping that my parents might let me go to school late so I wouldn't have to get up so early and rush around. My mom figured that out right away.

"Harry, I bet an important chess king like yourself thinks that getting up should be done later in the morning so that you can be totally rested when you make the grand entrance. The way I see it, we need to get an important person like you out there as early as we can so the fans don't have to wait."

I could hear my dad busting up in the background. I knew there was no way I was going to be allowed to sleep late.

"The good news is that your mother has agreed to drive you to school, Harry," my father called out from the kitchen. I dragged myself out of the bed and before I even made it to the bathroom, the phone had already started ringing again. I could hear each of my parents calling out at the same time, "I'll get it!"

My mom drove me to school and seemed very upbeat. When I got to school the cafeteria was full of kids and Mrs. Starck was waiting at the door. I walked in and everyone started to clap; Tommy was out of control. The "Good Luck, Harry" banner that had been in my classroom was now in the cafeteria with a new one underneath it which said, "Harry Jones wins Kings of K–12 Chess Tournament." Jack was standing under it pointing up to the words and had this huge, and I mean huge, grin on his face. I think I was almost more excited than I was the day I won. Before the classes were dismissed to their rooms, Mrs. Starck got on the microphone and congratulated me, explaining to the younger children what this was all about. She said that we would be having a special school assembly to talk about it.

It seemed that my mom was never going to leave my school that day. She hung around talking to Mrs. Lamont while we all did our usual morning exercises. I could still hear her voice as we all sat in our morning circle to share. Jack was the first one to join the circle, which was not like him at all. Tommy wandered around telling everyone who wasn't in the circle already to hurry up and get over there. Normally, Mrs. Lamont would say something to him or give him her "raise the eyebrow

15

look," but not this day. This day was different. Our sharing seemed to go on forever and Mrs. Starck even popped in for some of it. I got to speak and then Jack did, too. Now, if you remember how uncomfortable Jack is in front of the whole class, you understand that this was really something. Just before we stopped, Mrs. Lamont asked me if there was anything about the tournament that was hard besides trying to win. My mind quickly flashed back to the look on Dawn's face as I made my last few moves and her wet eyes when the tournament was over. This would be the first time that I really got to talk about it.

"Should I share this or keep it to myself?" I wondered. I decided to share it since other kids might also have this same kind of experience someday.

"Well, there was one part of the whole tournament that was really hard," I began. "I had to play against this girl named Dawn, who had become a close chess friend. She had helped me get into the group, and in a way, she was my cheerleader. She ended up doing what she told me not to do and I think that helped me to win the tournament. Dawn is as good at chess as me and I still can't believe that she lost and I won. It made winning kind of hard, if you know what I mean."

Mrs. Lamont asked the class if anyone else had ever had a similar experience and I was amazed at how many hands went up. Mostly it had to do with some kind of sport, but listening to the other kids talk made me realize that it happens a lot.

My first day back went pretty fast, especially since we only had a few weeks of school left and were ending some study units. I felt like a famous person most of the day and by lunchtime I was pretty tired. But when it was time to get on the bus and see my friend Jeb, I was excited all over again. Mr. Barrett, our bus driver, was so happy that he got off the bus as soon as he saw me, which I don't think he was supposed to do. He gave me this "hugshake," which Jeb says is a combination of a hug and a handshake. Mr. Barrett likes to shake your hand and hug you all at the same time! Once I managed to move up the steps, Jeb and the rest of the kids on the bus started hooting and clapping. Jeb is usually not on the bus on Mondays, but he promised me when I left that if I won the tournament he'd be on the bus the first day I got back. And there he was.

The ride back to Boston went so fast that when it was time for me to get off, I thought Mr. Barrett had made a mistake.

"Come on you famous young man. This is your stop. Your day is over," he said.

"Bye, Mr. Barrett," I called out as I went skipping down the steps of the bus. As I raced home, I thought to myself, "What a day this has been."

Grampy was waiting on the steps when I came around the corner and Mr. Peace was standing there with his dog, Old Blue. Mr. Peace lives next door. He spends most of his time walking Old Blue. I've spent a lot of my time tripping over Old Blue, who is very old and so blind that he doesn't move out of anybody's way.

"Hi, Mr. Peace. Hey, Old Blue, how are ya?" I called out as I leaned over and patted Old Blue. I could feel the dog immediately moving up against my body for more.

"Congratulations, Harry. Your Grampy tells me I have a chess king living next door to me now. You've got this whole neighborhood excited about chess. I don't even know what the game is all about and I'm excited about it, Harry. This is big stuff, son."

I think that was the most Mr. Peace had ever said to me. It sure made me feel proud. I could tell that Grampy had gone through every detail with Mr. Peace so I decided to let Grampy keep telling the story while I went in and got my snack.

"Great to see you, Mr. Peace," I called out as I ran up the steps to our apartment.

"Harry, your mama is at the grocery store but she said she made you some brownies," Grampy yelled. "They're on the counter next to the stove. She also said that people have been calling her asking questions about you and wanting to take pictures. Your mama will tell you all about it when she comes home."

I wanted to ask Grampy more questions about the phone calls, but I could tell that he was really into telling Mr. Peace about the tournament.

"Thanks, Grampy. Sounds great!"

When I got upstairs I saw that my mother had taken a lot of telephone messages and had questions written down that I think the callers wanted me to answer. It was pretty clear that Mom didn't know a lot about chess. Just as I bit into my first brownie, I heard her calling me to help carry the bags of groceries upstairs.

"Before you were famous, you were strong, Harry, so bring those strong arms down here and help me get these bags upstairs," she called.

I stuffed a brownie into my mouth and ran down to help her. Before I even got my arms around a bag, Mom started telling me about all the people who had called. Some man from one of the city papers asked if he could stop by and take my picture. Then a woman from one of our community papers wanted to take my picture after school one day. Two other people called from local chess clubs asking if I wanted to stop by over the weekend and talk to the young players about how neat it is to play chess. And then someone from a chess magazine in New York wanted to interview me over the phone.

My mom was on autopilot and she just kept on talking while I was trying to get two very heavy bags upstairs. I could hear Grampy in the background saying good-bye to Mr. Peace so I knew he was on his way up to hear what was going on. Just as Grampy got up the stairs, I could hear my dad coming in. And if that wasn't enough, the doorbell and the phone rang at the same time.

Herbie and Hank were at the door as was the man from the local newspaper wanting to take my picture. I could tell that Herbie was kind of hoping to be in the photo, too, but I knew that would never happen. The newspaperman told us right from the start that he had only ten minutes and he just wanted a picture of me in front of my chessboard. I think Grampy was even more disappointed than Herbie about not being in the picture and I could hear him saying in the background, "Well I'm the one who plays chess with Harry when he gets home from school. I'm his Grampy and they've played chess in my family for generations."

The man from the paper just smiled, shot the picture, asked me a few questions, and left. My dad called out to him as he was leaving to find out when they would run the photo.

Once everyone calmed down, Herbie and Hank had a snack with me and then Mom sent them on their way. I was kind of glad because I was so tired. I felt like I was on an escalator that kept moving faster and faster, with no place to jump off. I was also beginning to understand what jet lag was all about. I was still on Colorado time, but my body had to run on Massachusetts time.

Dinner was pretty funny. It seemed as if everyone had so much to say that I almost had to raise my hand to get the floor. It was just like school! We were all very tired, but we were as excited as we were tired so it was pretty funny. I was trying to figure out how I would ever have the energy to do my homework.

I just kept thinking about how good my bed would feel. My parents took care of that thought pretty fast when they both announced, "Harry, no more phone or friends tonight. Time for homework."

It sure didn't take long to get back to reality. Grampy always loves that I have homework and he doesn't. He always adds his favorite, "My homework is to relax, Harry, so I'll just find a comfortable chair since I already did fourth grade."

I was glad that Mrs. Lamont had given us a light load. The year was winding down and we were finishing up a science project that I loved and also working on our Egypt reports. I had done all my research and was just editing my work, so it moved along pretty easily. Mrs. Lamont had announced that in celebration of my winning the tournament, we were all going to write about a time in our lives when we got really excited about something special. It could be anything—a birthday present, a Christmas play, having someone special come visit, anything that got us excited.

My homework didn't go very quickly, but when I started to write about the tournament, I got so excited that I had this burst of energy and went into high gear. I felt as if I was writing too much. I could hear Mrs. Lamont saying, "Don't put information in that is unimportant to the story." We all seem to ramble and she wants longer sentences that are "rich with important information." I know all her favorite phrases. She asks us to repeat them on a regular basis. Tommy says we are "teacher's parrots," which is different from "teacher's pets." Tommy has his own way with words.

When I had said good night to everyone and it was time to shut my light off, I was so wired about what I had written about the tournament that I couldn't fall asleep. It was fun reliving it, but this time every detail was there. Even stuff that I hadn't much thought about, like the moment when I realized all the special people in my life were there at the tournament. I couldn't believe that all this had happened to me, Harry Jones.

Chapter Four

“**H**arry, wake up now. Your alarm went off ten minutes ago. Today you have to take the bus, so you better get moving. Come on now, tell your bed you'll be back tonight!” said my mom being kind of a jokester.

I dragged myself out of bed and moved into high gear. I was very late and I knew Mr. Barrett would be at the corner in twenty minutes. I rushed through breakfast, quickly made my bed, and raced out the door, past Grampy, who I could tell was ready for a quick chat. Mr. Peace and Old Blue were out there, too, and before I even got to Old Blue he started howling like a hunting dog. There are some things that never, ever change and Old Blue is one of them.

When I got to the corner, the bus was just pulling up and Mr. Barrett had that “you just made it” look on his face. He stopped the bus but didn't open the door right away. Instead, he was looking in his mirror at the kids on the bus and saying something to them. When he finally opened the door, everyone started cheering and clapping. I had forgotten that some of the kids who usually ride with me hadn't been there yesterday afternoon. Mr. Barrett was enjoying every minute of it. He was a lot like my Grampy except instead of sitting on a front stoop, he sat in the driver's seat of a bus.

Jeb was in the back waiting for me, but it took me a while to settle in and talk to him. About halfway to school things finally quieted down and I got to visit with Jeb.

Since school was winding down for the year, one of the things we talked about was summer. I hadn't even thought about my summer. Jeb was traveling down to Georgia to visit his grandparents and then he was going to attend two basketball camps. He seemed excited that summer was right around the corner. I had been so busy with the chess tournament that I had hardly thought much about it.

This was my first summer as a chess player and I had heard that there were some great chess camps not too far away. Last summer I had gone to hockey camp and practiced most of the month of August. I suddenly realized that this summer I would have to think about whether I would go back to hockey or continue with chess. The doctor said I could start skating again, slowly, by the end of summer and could rejoin my team in the fall. At the time, fall seemed really far away but now it was closer than I wanted it to be. Deciding between the two things you love the most is not easy and I was kind of hoping that I wouldn't have to make a choice. Maybe I'd be able to do both.

When the bus pulled up to the school cafeteria door, Tommy was waiting for me and I could see Jack racing across the playground. Jeb started laughing and joking about my fan club. I really liked my school and the trip from Boston didn't really bother me very much anymore. A lot had changed and I think my fourth-grade year was the best ever in school.

Tommy, Jack, and I hung out at our table in the cafeteria before going down to our classroom. While we were waiting, some of the students from other classes wandered over and asked me questions about chess and the tournament. Some just came over and congratulated me.

Mrs. Lamont was waiting at our door with her usual smile and upbeat "Good morning, everyone." Each morning she was like a recording reminding us about our homework and anything else we needed to bring into the class. Each time she said it, it was like she had never said it before. I wondered how she could do the same thing everyday and love it so much, but Grampy said that we all end up doing pretty much the same thing everyday. I suppose that's right.

We were completing units in reading, spelling, math, and science and not starting anything new. Even in art, we were completing a big mural about our years at the Mercier School. In the section I was helping to draw, Jack, Tommy, and I were playing chess with the chess club banner in the background. Tommy and Jack wanted me to add the tournament but it didn't happen at school so I told them it didn't belong on the mural. Mrs. Lamont worked on a memory chart with us in class, which was also a lot of fun. Tommy's memory was about the day he found real friends. I had always thought that the problem was about not living near your friends, but I learned through Tommy that you can go to a school your whole life and not be close to anyone. He must have been just as lonely as I was, maybe even more so because I had Herbie and Hank. I still wished that we could all be in the same school, but I have learned that a lot of kids go to schools other than those in their neighborhoods.

First thing Saturday morning our doorbell rang. I was sure it was Herbie, but when I opened it I was surprised to find my hockey coach standing there.

"I just wanted to stop by and congratulate you, Harry," Coach Miller said. "I saw your picture in the paper and we posted it in the locker room so all your teammates can see it when they come back for practice in August."

"Thanks, Coach Miller. I really miss seeing all the guys at practice. I can't remember the last time I had my skates on which is weird because I seemed to have them on all the time before my injury," I replied.

Coach Miller smiled but then he got this kind of serious look on his face. "Practice starts up in mid-August, Harry, and we still have a spot for you. Hopefully, you can play both chess and hockey."

Before I got to answer, my dad piped in.

"We really appreciate your holding a place for Harry. He's got to think about all this and how he's going to spend his summer. He's a lucky boy to have so many choices and to have his coach come to see him."

Coach Miller smiled and agreed with my dad that I had a lot to think about. I was glad my dad had spoken up since I had no idea what I wanted to do. I was hoping I might be able to do both, but I was kind of worried about how much that would cost. I really needed to talk with my parents.

Coach Miller stayed and had coffee with us and talked about the past season. My dad thanked him for including me in the banquet and for all the phone calls to see how I was doing. Of course, as soon as Grampy came in the conversation went from hockey to the chess tournament. I think Coach Miller finally left because the talk was all about chess.

The weekend went by pretty fast. I got to spend Saturday night watching a movie over at Herbie's. Hank was there, too. As always, Herbie's house had more going on in it at one time than any house I have ever been to. His brothers came in one by one and congratulated me on the chess tournament. Each time one of them came in, Herbie would pause the movie and give this big sigh. Hank would look at him and say, "Get over it, Herbie. They just want to hear about the tournament. The movie will keep." Herbie just rolled his eyes and gave out one of those sighs that sounds more like a painful groan from Old Blue.

Finally the movie was over and Herbie's oldest brother walked Hank and me home, with Herbie trailing behind. Even though Herbie always acts like his brothers are one big pain, he really looks up to each one of them.

I was hoping to sleep late on Sunday morning, but church won. I could tell my parents were really excited to go and I was kind of excited myself. Our congregation was like our extended family and I knew they'd be thanking the good Lord that I had done so well at the tournament. At the social hour after services, the pastor came over and told me that he was also a chess player and that he used to play with his grampy all the time. I kind of wished that my Grampy had come to the service to hear this himself, but church was something that he occasionally passed on. He always tells us that he already has all God's blessings and then some.

Chapter Five

S chool was almost over. We only had about ten days left. For the first time the ending of school made me kind of sad. Seeing Jack would be more complicated once school got out since we lived so far away from each other. I'd miss Tommy, too. The three of us had become really good friends. I felt pretty lucky because I had Hank and Herbie in Boston, and Tommy and Jack out at school. Some kids don't have any friends, and I had four really close ones.

The weather was moving into summer so it was kind of hard to concentrate. Recess seemed too short and our classwork went on forever. During recess it wasn't just Tommy and Jack and I playing chess anymore. Other kids would come over and watch the whole game. It was kind of weird and at first I wasn't sure if I liked it.

Tommy was the one who noticed it, and then Jack. The little corner of the playground that we went to was no longer our own special place. It had become everybody's place.

By the end of our last full week of school, everyone seemed to be annoying me. My mother was really on my case to get up on time and look good. Grampy kept trying to talk to me while I was supposed to be dressing, and I got rushed out the door so fast for the bus that I hardly got any breakfast.

"Is this how you treat a 'chess king?'" I thought to myself.

At school, there was even more rushing. Mrs. Starck, our principal, had called a special assembly during our gym time.

Our class went last to the assembly, which was definitely a first. I thought Mrs. Lamont had forgotten about it, but then the office called us down. They kept announcing individual rooms rather than just "time for fourth grade." Mrs. Lamont asked me to go to the end of the line and I wasn't even talking, so Tommy and Jack got to be next to each other and I had to go to the back.

"What is this?" I thought to myself getting more and more annoyed.

I noticed the school superintendent and his assistant coming in the back door of our school while we were lining up to go into the assembly. Mrs. Starck always invited them to very special assemblies, like the time we had one for the Mercier Movers, the school chess club. Then I saw them coming toward me with big smiles on their faces.

"Whoa, I thought to myself, what is this all about?"

"Harry, congratulations. We understand you have won a very impressive chess tournament. We hear that this is quite something to win the very first major tournament that you enter and to accomplish so much in so little time," said the superintendent.

As I was shaking his hand, Tommy was waving me inside. I peeked in and there in the front of the cafeteria was the Mercier Movers banner. The kids had made posters that were hanging up all over one side of the cafeteria. They said things like, "Awesome Job," "Go, Harry." On the other side were posters congratulating our third graders for getting first place in the town's food drive. The parents of the third graders were there. We had quite a crowd, but even with all those people I could hear a familiar voice cheering. I knew it had to be my Grampy. My parents were at his side, but no one could hoot and holler like my Grampy when something special was happening. I remembered when my family had come to school earlier in the year on the day we announced the Mercier Movers to everyone.

After the Pledge of Allegiance, Mrs. Starck introduced the kids who had been so great at getting lots of food for the town's food pantry. They all stood up and faced us; everyone cheered and clapped. Then the head of the food pantry spoke about the importance of providing food for everyone to eat well. Then she went on to say how much work it is for the classroom teachers to organize the collection and how much time it takes to check all the food and pack it up. She especially thanked the parents of the students for being so generous, and of course the biggest thank-you was to the students for bringing the food in each day. Some had given up dessert and allowance to buy extra food to donate.

Chapter Five

Then she announced that there was something else to celebrate, a first for Mercier. She called out my name on the microphone and asked me to come up to the front.

I could hear Tommy's and my Grampy's cheers and whistles, but what really struck me were the faces of the younger students. They seemed to be studying me as though I were going to say something very important. Suddenly I got really nervous.

"What was I going to say?" I thought to myself. I needed someone to help me out and there was no one there to do that. The only person that could help me was me! I could feel my stomach getting tighter and tighter.

Mrs. Starck calmed everyone down and gave a little speech about how I had gotten injured in hockey and made the best of it by trying something new. She gave a little background about how I played chess with my dad and my Grampy, and sometimes my friends. Then she talked about how much courage it took for me to accept my hockey injury and then to compete in chess tournaments. She mentioned our April assembly and how Tommy, Jack, and I had come up with the idea of a chess club at Mercier, and how great it was to have even younger students asking about chess. Then she explained a little about the Kings of K–12 Chess Tournament and how my family and I had gone all the way to Colorado. Just when I was feeling pretty relaxed and totally convinced that Mrs. Starck was going to do all the talking, she gave the microphone to me and everyone started clapping and cheering all over again. What came out of my mouth really surprised me.

"It's kind of weird how I ended up playing in chess tournaments since hockey is what I really wanted to be doing," I began. "I was pretty upset when they said I couldn't play hockey. I thought I wouldn't be cool anymore because I got injured. Then my friend Jack showed up with a chess set and that kind of changed all the bad stuff for me. Going on a plane to Colorado with other kids was really neat, but it was really great having my dad and my Grampy with me. Winning the tournament and having the rest of my family surprise me out there was awesome. The best was having my friend Jack there, too. And then, after all that, my hockey coach asked me to come back and play hockey again. This is really cool, but kind of confusing. Now I have two choices and I don't know which one to take. I guess what I've learned is that there are lots of choices. I'm glad I know how to play chess and that I was able to get over being so upset about not playing hockey for the season. Sometimes things just work out, even when you don't think they will."

After I finished, I could feel my face getting kind of red and hot. Mrs. Starck thanked me and then talked to all the Mercier students about the summer and how she hoped that one of our choices would be reading. She ended the assembly by reciting a very funny poem about a silly summer vacation that never really happened. I think she was trying to tell us that we can make our own vacations. Tommy looked totally confused and the kindergarteners were really giggling, so I'm pretty sure they didn't get it.

When I got home from school, instead of being really excited about the assembly I was feeling kind of down. The excitement of winning and being a famous chess king was over and pretty soon school would be over, too. I had lots of chess options, camps to go to and tutoring opportunities at chess events, plenty to keep me busy.

"What's wrong with me?" I thought to myself.

I kept thinking about two things: Dawn's surgery and hockey camp. I knew Dawn was about to have her scoliosis surgery and I hadn't really talked to her or seen her since Colorado. I knew how badly she had wanted to win the tournament and I think she was a lot more disappointed than she let on. Usually she e-mailed me, but I hadn't heard from her in almost two weeks and I was feeling kind of sad about that. I guess I was wondering if she was mad because I won and she didn't.

The other thing on my mind was hockey. I was hearing a lot of my classmates talking about their summer hockey camps and I was starting to think about hockey more and more. I didn't tell my parents because they were so hot on chess that they didn't seem to care about hockey anymore.

I could hear someone at my door and I really didn't feel like opening it.

"Harry, can I come in?" my mom whispered. "You seemed kind of quiet tonight and I heard you tell Hank and Herbie that you didn't want to go out with them. Is everything all right, Harry?"

"Yeah! Everything's great, Mom. I'm just tired, that's all."

"Well, you've had a pretty exciting day, Harry Jones," she chuckled.

I smiled back at her, but I knew that she could tell I wasn't feeling very excited at all.

"Talk to me, Harry. There's something up with you; you're just not yourself, son."

"I'm fine, Mom. I'm just tired and I'm kind of sad about school getting out," I answered.

"Well, I can understand that, Harry. You've made a lot of new and wonderful friends this year at Mercier and I know that you think it's always harder to see them when school is not in session because of the distance. That's not really true because they can come for overnights, Harry, and you also have e-mail."

I couldn't even answer. I had nothing to say.

"Harry, is that the only thing that's bothering you?" my mom asked.

"Mom, I don't know what I want to do this summer," I replied, "and I have about a week to decide. I should be excited about the chess activities, but I just don't know if that's what I want to do all summer."

"Wait a minute, Harry," my mom broke in. "Who said that you had to do chess all summer? I didn't hear anyone say that to you. Maybe that's what you *think* you have to do because you've done so well at chess."

"But Mom. Chess is all you and Dad talk to me about. Even Grampy. He never says anything about anything but chess these days."

My mom looked very serious and kind of confused. Then she got a big smile on her face and gave me this strange look.

"Harry, we thought that's what you wanted to talk about. You never tell us about anything else. You know parents are kind of like trained seals, we just talk about what we think our children want us to talk about," Mom said.

"I kind of miss hearing about hockey, myself." I looked up and my dad was standing in the doorway of my room.

"Tell us what you want to talk about, Harry," said Dad, "not what you think we want to hear."

My dad just stood there waiting for me to answer him. My mom was quiet, too. I almost felt like I was going to cry. Then I just blurted it all out.

"How come Dawn doesn't e-mail me anymore. Is that what it means to win a chess game? You win the game and you lose your friend. And why can't I play hockey and chess? I like both of them and I don't know what I want to do anymore."

"Harry, Harry, Harry," my mom said. "Dawn and her family are still traveling and won't be home until Sunday. Her parents told us this at the competition. They planned to visit all the national parks. Nobody is mad at anybody. They're just away. Dawn's surgery is next week so they took a vacation beforehand."

"Why didn't you tell me that?" I asked, kind of annoyed.

"Harry, I didn't tell you because you never brought it up, that's why. I was sure that Dawn had told you, but of course you were both so busy with the tournament that you didn't have time to think or talk about anything else. I am so sorry you did all this worrying for no reason."

She was right. I did know but I guess I had forgotten in all the excitement of the return to Boston and the ending of school.

"Harry, what about hockey?" my dad asked. "Are you worried that it is too expensive to do both chess and hockey?"

"Well, yeah, kind of, Dad," I answered. "And even if I could do both, I don't know what I want to do."

"Harry, give it some time. You have a few days to decide about the chess camp. Maybe you don't even want to go to chess camp. How about just giving yourself a little time and exploring both the chess and the hockey? It's okay to want to do both of them, son, and it's also okay not to want to do either or just one of them. Only you can decide all this."

"Well, why don't I know what I want to do, Dad? How come I am so good at chess and I'm feeling so bad about everything else right now? I just don't get it. I'm feeling so confused about everything."

"Sometimes, Harry," said my dad, "there's a letdown when all the excitement is over. It happens to adults, too. Winning that chess tournament was a very big deal. Now it's over and on top of that, it's hard leaving school and having some of your friends so far from where we live. I'm sure that you're not the only one feeling this way. Just give it some time, son, and I think it will all work out. Don't put so much pressure on yourself to decide right now. Just wait until you're able to think more clearly."

When my mom and dad left, I decided to e-mail Dawn and wish her luck with her surgery and tell her what I was thinking. I should have just gone ahead and done this earlier in the week. I kind of wished that I could talk to her on the phone and tell her.

I wanted to understand a little bit more about Dawn's scoliosis since I still didn't know very much. I wanted to know how her scoliosis was different from mine and if it wasn't, how come she needed surgery and I didn't? Maybe I was gonna need it and no one was telling me. Oh, wow, I really wanted to get out of the funk I was in and start to feel better about things. Even after my hockey injury, I wasn't feeling this confused. I was pretty down then, but I wasn't confused.

Chapter Six

I woke up Saturday morning to find Herbie standing over me wondering why I wasn't out of bed yet. He and Hank were going over to the park to shoot some hoops and they needed one more person. Before I knew it, I was out of bed, dressed, and trying to eat breakfast, with Herbie asking me every minute if I was going to finish my griddlecakes. My mom had already given him a plate of his own, but he wolfed them down so fast that my mom told him his body wouldn't even have a clue that the food had entered.

On the way to the park, Herbie told me that a famous hockey guy was speaking over at the university where I had played my hockey games, and if I wanted, even though I wasn't playing right now, he could get me in to hear him. Herbie's brother had gotten tickets for Hank and him and he could get another one for me. Herbie's brother was really into hockey and even though Herbie always said, "Hockey, smockey," I knew that he loved watching his brother play, and anyone else, too. Herbie would have been a good player himself, but being the youngest of four boys he decided not to try. Anyway, I told him I would think about going and let him know after lunch.

When we got to the basketball court, Hank was already pretty sweaty and so I could tell that he had been there a while. Hank and Herbie loved basketball and their favorite thing was Saturday hoops. We played for a long time and when we finished I had forgotten all about my Friday night. Things were cool. I was even getting excited about summer and the idea that in less than a week we could come out here and play hoops whenever we wanted. We usually went to the Boy's Club for summer sports, but when we didn't do that, we hung out at the park. I really loved where I lived and the energy that the city gave off was something that people in the country had a hard time appreciating. Many of them thought of the city as a dangerous place and that was not true at all. It was just a place that had more people in it and so you had to be smart about what you did. My dad always says that you have to learn about your "environment," wherever you live. That was something he taught my sister and me from the time we were old enough to understand.

After basketball we all went for a quick lunch. While we were eating, Herbie and Hank convinced me to go with them to the university that night. Hank said the speaker was a former Boston Bruin who had suffered some serious injuries and finally had to give up the sport when he was at the top of his career. Hank always liked to follow all this stuff and sometimes he sounded like my dad when he was explaining things. I kind of thought I knew who the hockey player was because my dad had mentioned him when I had my injury last fall. To be honest, I couldn't have given a rat's tail last fall about hearing him, but now I was really kind of excited about his story.

I called my parents from the Boy's Club to see if it was okay if I went with Herbie and Hank. I didn't have any plans and they both seemed pretty excited that I was going to hear the speaker. Herbie's mom also invited me to dinner. I went home to shower and then my dad walked me over to Herbie's to see if he could help out and drive us one way to the university, but Herbie's brothers had it under control.

Chapter Six

Dinner at Herbie's was like an assembly line since his mother always cooked for a large crowd. She had made meatballs and sauce, plus sub rolls, and a big salad. We all lined up in the kitchen with our plates. Herbie's brothers had their friends over, too, and one of his brothers even had a girlfriend visiting. I was amazed at how relaxed his mother was about feeding what looked to me like an army.

After dinner we all piled in different cars and went off to the university, which is kind of the same as a college, but a little different, too. Don't ask me how they're different, but if they weren't, Grampy says they'd have the same name. Anyway, once we got to the university, it took us about fifteen minutes to get in the door and up to our seats in the top rows. I couldn't believe how crowded it was. It was very cool when the lights went off and the speaker came out under the spotlight. For me it was both kind of exciting and weird since the last time I was at this rink I left in an ambulance. And here I was about to hear somebody else's hockey story.

When the speaker came out, behind him up on a huge TV screen was his Bruins' jersey. The crowd went nuts. His eyes kind of got real glassy and shiny-looking and you could tell that he wished he was still on the ice. I felt like he and I had this special connection, even though we didn't know each other. Once everyone quieted down, he began to speak. First he talked about hockey and how hard he had worked his whole life to get to be on the Bruins. He said that if you want to be good at anything, you really have to work hard and you have to want it really badly. Then he talked about school and how his hockey coaches always made him and all his team members do their homework or else they couldn't play in the games. He told us that he knew that school was as important as hockey. After that he showed us movies of his time with the Bruins and, finally, a tape of his last game. He talked about being injured and how he felt when he first found out how bad his injury was. Just before his last game, he even took time off, hoping that he would get better and be able to play again. When he went back on the ice, he knew that it just wasn't going to work and he would have to give it up. He talked about the messages that our bodies send to us and how important it is to listen so that we don't hurt ourselves permanently. He also said that this isn't just about hockey; it is true about any sport.

Just when I thought he was done, he started up a whole new talk about outlets and how we can still make a difference in the world, even when we have to give up something we really love. He asked his brother, who was sitting out in the audience, to come up and join him at the microphone. He talked about how he and his brother and sisters, who were not there, had grown up in Canada and how they were all big supporters of helping people who had cancer. He said that they did this because of their parents and that he hoped to build an apartment in a hospital to give people a place to stay while their family member was getting what he called "treatment." He explained that treatment was what they do to try to help people with cancer get better. He said that when he couldn't play hockey anymore, he and his brother decided to work really hard to make their dream about an apartment in a hospital come true. His brother spoke a little bit about their dream and then they told everyone where donations could be sent to help them with this big idea. Then, his brother gave the microphone back and the great player ended by saying how much he still loved hockey with all his heart and how he wished that he could still play on a team. He explained that he had joined a different team and it was all about helping and healing families who are touched by cancer. The audience went wild when he finished and everyone stood up and clapped louder than any crowd I had ever heard. He wasn't just a famous hockey player; he had become much more.

What really stuck in my head was that he kept saying how important it is not to ever give up, even when you can't do something that you really love. He talked about ways that all of us can make a difference, even when we think we aren't doing anything really great.

So many of the things he talked about I had felt the night I got injured. I couldn't believe that a big, famous guy like him could feel all the same stuff. It made me want to go up and touch him and tell him my own story, but I knew that he had probably heard a lot of stories like mine.

After the talk, Herbie's brother said I could stand in line and try to get an autograph. The line practically circled the whole gym area, and I ended up waiting for a very long time. When I finally got up to the player, he looked like a giant, and he made me feel like he had known me before. Herbie was with me, and as the speaker started to sign my program, Herbie yelled out, "Ya know he had an injury, too, and now he can play again but he's not sure he wants to."

As the speaker was handing me my signed program, he took it back and wrote one more thing under his name. As I walked away I read it, "If you can, get back on the ice! Good luck. C.N." I just couldn't believe it and I was glad that Herbie had opened his big mouth. I never would have had the courage to tell C.N. myself.

By the time I got home it was after midnight and not one but both of my parents were waiting at the door. I was sure I was in big trouble, but instead they told me that Herbie's big brother had called and they wanted to hear all about the evening. Then my mom added, "Remember, it's late so give us the short version, Harry. We're tired."

I ended up telling them almost his whole speech and I could see that my mom was as excited as my dad. Then I told them about Herbie telling C.N. about my injury and showed them what he had written on my program.

By the time I went to bed, I was so excited that I could hardly get to sleep. If the rink had been open, I think I would have put on my skates and gone right over and practiced. I had this unbelievable energy inside me and I just wanted to get out and use it, right then and there.

On Sunday, I slept until almost lunchtime and when I got up, Mom was at church and Dad and Grampy were playing chess. My bed still looked good to me, but my stomach sounded like there was a battle going on so I knew I needed to find some food. My dad offered to make me some eggs so I ended up sitting in for my dad at the chessboard and figuring out his next move while he cooked for me. Grampy had already heard about the big night and how the speaker had signed my program twice, all because of Herbie. Grampy got all excited and I think he was hoping I would get distracted and he'd win the game, but no such luck. I ended up distracting him, instead, and I won. Grampy made sure I knew that this was the last time I was going to be allowed to take over for my dad. We all ended up laughing about it, although Grampy still looked pretty bummed.

I was so tired that I spent the rest of the day just hanging out and relaxing. Mom had to work the three-to-eleven shift at the hospital so we all just hung around and didn't do much of anything.

When dinnertime came, Dad asked me if I wanted to walk down the street and get a pizza. I think he was as tired of the TV as me. It was a big treat to order out. My dad is a good cook and he can make a dinner almost as well as my mom. Grampy didn't want to come and just asked us to bring some pizza home for him. I had the feeling that my dad wanted to talk to me alone so he didn't push Grampy. We weren't five minutes out the door when he began.

"Harry, I've been doing some research on chess and hockey. I think I have found two things that you might be interested in. There is a Grandmaster who lives in Boston and runs private chess lessons. He is known as a chess guru and he gives chess lessons to students as young as six years old and private lessons to adults as old as sixty. He had an ad on his website looking for chess players who were interested in donating some time and helping him with the less experienced players. I called him and he said that he would be willing to give you some private lessons in exchange for your help with the other students.

"Harry, I've also done some hockey research for you. There is a summer league at your old practice rink that meets once a week. They have a special clinic for players returning after an injury. Even though you're a few years younger than these players, the coach said he would be willing to have you join the group and he would work up a program to help you get your strength back. He's a good friend of Coach Miller and he said that he would talk to Coach Miller to make sure he set up the right program for you."

I could tell that my dad had put a lot of time into this and I really did appreciate his hard work, but I wanted some time to think about it all. The chess thing sounded pretty good and so did going back to hockey. I knew I really wanted to do both, but I was still afraid of the boards and I knew that I couldn't be a good player if I spent my whole time back on the ice staying away from boards. I wasn't sure what to do.

"Dad, I really appreciate all your hard work," I said. "I just want some time to think about it before I give you an answer. I hope that's okay with you."

"No problem, son. I just want you to have a good summer and be happy. And I really want you to understand that you *can* do both, Harry. The chess is free because you'll be helping out, kind of like a tutor, and the summer hockey league is very fairly priced. It only meets once a week."

"Thanks a lot, Dad. I promise to think it over in the next few days and let you know. I'm just kind of tired today so I don't want to have to think about anything," I answered.

When we got to the pizza place it seemed as though the whole neighborhood were there. It was fun to chat with everyone and it seemed more like a pizza party than just ordering out. Sometimes we take it home, but this time we decided not to. We found an empty booth and started to eat.

When we got home, I went right to my e-mail to send one last note off to Dawn. I could tell by the e-mail she had sent me when she arrived back home from her trip that she was getting pretty nervous about the operation. Jack had also sent me an e-mail about an overnight on the last day of school and I also had a message from Consuela. By the time I finished answering everyone, it was time to shower and get ready to go to bed and do my reading. On the weekends I was allowed to read whatever I wanted as long as I reported on it. I remembered back to the days when I hated to read. Now, I really like it, especially when I can choose my own stuff. But I don't always like all the school reading assignments.

"Hi, son. I just thought I'd come in and say good night and tell you how happy I am that what started as a bad weekend for you, ended up, I hope, as a good one."

"Thanks, Dad. It really was a good weekend."

"Harry, I hope that when you go back on the ice, you can stop worrying about hitting the boards again. Coach Miller says that your summer league coach can help you with this and that it's not unusual to be a little nervous. It's up to you whether you play or not, Harry, but I hope you don't decide against it because of the boards."

"Thanks, Dad. I know you want to talk some more, but I really just want to go to bed."

"No problem, son. Have a good sleep. I enjoyed the pizza tonight."

Once the light went out, I lay in my bed for what seemed like a long, long time thinking about what my dad had said. I *was* afraid of the boards. Who wouldn't be after an injury like mine? What bothered me the most was that I still didn't know how it had happened. I was always pretty careful on the ice and I often think about that game and wonder what I did differently during that night. I wish I had a video so I could look back and really see how I ended up where I did. But as nervous as I was about playing again, most of me was ready to get back on the ice.

Chapter Seven

My last few days of school went by very fast and it seemed as if our class had something happening every minute. It had gotten really, really hot so I was happy about the Popsicles our room mother supplied. For the first time ever, I was sad about the school year being over. Jack, Tommy, and I promised each other that we would keep in touch over the summer. Other kids had said that other years, but this time it was different. I knew they really meant it.

On the very last day of school, Jack invited Tommy and me for an overnight and his parents brought us to Walden Pond. We had lots of choices of activities and the first thing Jack and I did was jump in the water. Tommy kind of hung on the edge. He said that he wasn't hot enough to swim. The water was kind of cool so Jack and I didn't think anything of it.

We had a picnic dinner and then we took a hike way up into the woods. Jack's dad knew a lot about the area around the pond so we all got a nature lesson, but he made it seem more like an adventure. Tommy was really getting into it and at times Jack and I couldn't help but laugh at how serious he was about it all. It was like we were in Mrs. Lamont's science class and it was Tommy's turn to ask questions. Jack's dad could hardly get the answers out fast enough.

When we got home it was late and we were allowed to stay up just a little bit longer and talk. We ended up discussing summer and what each of us would be doing.

Jack was really excited about the overnight camp he was going to. I wasn't sure I would be happy being away from my family for eight weeks, but Jack said that the time went by really fast and that he loved all the things they did at camp. Tommy's summer was sort of undecided, kind of like mine. He would probably do a lot of the town activities and then he was hoping to attend a basketball camp and a soccer camp. The basketball camp was overnight for a week at a local college. It was a big deal for Tommy since he had never gone before and he had gotten a scholarship from some organization in town. He was very, very proud that he had been chosen. I ended up talking to Tommy and Jack for a long time about my own summer plans, which kind of didn't exist. I just didn't know what I wanted to do. Both Tommy and Jack said that I should try the summer hockey league. Then Jack's dad came in and said it was time to "hit the sack."

When Tommy's parents and my mom and dad came to pick us up, they all decided we should have a beach day sometime in late August before school started up. At first Tommy's parents didn't say much and then finally his mom explained that she and his dad didn't know how to swim so they never took Tommy to the beach. Tommy looked down at the floor when they said that until my mom spoke up and said that she was a little afraid of the water herself. It all made sense, why Tommy had stayed at the edge of the water. He didn't want Jack and me to know that he couldn't swim. Jack's dad suggested that we go to a freshwater place like Walden Pond so that there was more to do than just swimming. By the time we left, it was all planned, including the date, the time, and the food.

Just as we were leaving, my mom asked Tommy and Jack if they wanted to come into the city for an overnight sometime in early July. She had forgotten that Jack would be leaving for overnight camp in just a few days. Tommy was really excited and even invited himself to one of my hockey practices. Of course, I hadn't even decided that I was going to try hockey again but that didn't matter to Tommy.

"Don't invite yourself to a practice or anything," Jack teased.

"Hey, Jack, I'm just trying to help Harry out. I figure if I invite myself to a practice, he'll have to start playing again," laughed Tommy.

"Either that or you'll need to find another kid who plays hockey and arrange to see him practice," dissed Jack.

"Okay! Okay! That's cool. I get it," answered Tommy.

My mom and dad burst out laughing and said that Tommy was definitely Herbie in another body.

After we said our good-byes, it was time to head on home to Beantown, which is a nickname for Boston. In the car my mom announced that she had a surprise. Consuela was home and she had brought someone with her for me to meet.

"Who is it?" I demanded.

"Well," my mom started, trying to hold back. "It's a dog and his name is Zeus."

"Zeus," I yelled out. "Since when does Consuela have a dog and who gave it a name like that?"

I guess Consuela had adopted Zeus from a foster-dog home. She never told my parents about it and her landlord said that Zeus had to go because one of the tenants had complained about his barking. Consuela had called Grampy all upset about giving Zeus back and so Grampy agreed to take him in. My parents didn't have much to say in it at all, which I think was Consuela's plan in the first place. I was really, really excited about having a dog around. My parents were kind of warm about it, but I couldn't wait to get home and meet Zeus. I almost forgot to be excited about seeing Consuela. She was totally awesome, but a dog was really, really cool.

When we arrived home, Grampy was sitting on the front step of our house with Zeus on one side and Consuela on the other. My mother was griping about who was going to walk the dog and who was going to do this and who was going to do that. Once we were out of the car, all was forgotten and the next thing I knew Zeus was laying kisses all over my mother's face. Then my dad got into it and I could hardly introduce myself to Zeus. I could not believe the welcome this dog was getting.

Zeus turned out to be a great dog, part black lab and part pointer. An eye infection had left his black fur almost gray around his sore eye. He looked kind of like he had a goggle around one eye. His tail was so long that it was like a whip and it almost put out one of Grampy's eyes. We all started laughing when Grampy told Zeus to control his tail, which seemed to make Zeus wag it even harder.

Having Consuela home for four days was the best. She had borrowed a friend's car and had driven up to deliver Zeus. Since it was such a long drive, she had decided to stay long enough to be sure Zeus adjusted.

I finally had someone I could really unload with about chess and hockey. We ended up having our talk over a chessboard since Consuela wanted to improve her game, which hardly existed to begin with. I realized while I was teaching her how much I enjoyed teaching the game and how much I really did love chess. But, I also kept thinking about hockey and how much I loved being out on the ice. Consuela convinced me that summer was a great time to do both and also to find out if maybe I could juggle them all year long.

By the time Consuela left, I think we had talked about every-thing from chess to hockey to scoliosis, with a lot of other stuff in the middle. I felt bad when she had to leave Zeus behind and say good-bye. Even though he was going to be very well cared for, he looked very sad about her leaving.

Zeus was an easygoing dog and within a few days it was as if he had been our dog for a long, long time. We were all very careful about not letting him slip out since we lived near a very busy street. Grampy was the most careful and he reminded us that Consuela was depending on her family to take good care of Zeus. No longer was I tripping over just Old Blue on the sidewalk. Now I had Zeus to get past, too.

Chapter Eight

A few days after Consuela left, my dad and I drove over to a new rink and I signed up for a summer hockey league that met once a week south of Boston. Coach Miller told my dad that our league had cancelled because not enough kids signed up so we had to join ranks with this other group. I guess the deal was that Boston would provide the coach and the other team would provide the ice. Good for them, but kind of weird for me to start out at a whole new rink with a lot of new kids. I was a little nervous because a lot of the players looked younger and I had a feeling that it was a beginner's league. I was pretty quiet on the way home and I think my dad knew I was kind of unhappy about it all. He tried to make me feel better by saying it might be good to start off with new players so that I wasn't so nervous and uncomfortable. I suppose he was right, but it had taken me four years of practice to make my team.

The same week I started hockey I became a chess tutor and helped a Grandmaster named Chetski teach chess to kids ranging in age from second grade through high school. Chetski rented space in one of the schools. He had two class-rooms: one had beginners in it and the other, experienced chess players. I had seen some of them at the matches and I was hoping that Chetski was going to teach this group himself since some of them were as good at chess as I am. I had e-mailed Dawn of my plans and she thought it was a great idea. She was really excited that I had decided to tutor chess, and even though she didn't know a lot about hockey, she said she thought I needed to go back to that, too. Then she went into this big thing about how we all need to follow our dreams and to try to do all the things that we want to do. It sounded like something my Grampy would say; kind of strange coming from someone my age but I knew what Dawn meant and I guess I would find out if she was right.

I took a bus over to start my chess tutoring. I was happy that I was able to find Chetski's classrooms on my own. He had for-gotten to put signs up so I think he was surprised when I found him.

"Hey man, what's shakin'? You must be Harry because I remember your picture from the chess magazine."

Chetski was a really neat guy, maybe in his early twenties, and he was very excited that I could help him. We figured out a schedule for the days that I would be there and also times when he and I could play some matches. He was very flexible, so everything seemed cool. While we waited for the kids to arrive, we started a match and he gave me a lesson on how he worked with beginners. I was glad he did this since I didn't even remember how I had begun learning the game. He explained that after I taught the kids how to set up the board, I needed to show them the chart he had made that told them the name of each piece and its job in the game. He wanted me to get the students to think about solving a problem or a mystery. The most important part of the game of chess is observation and thinking about what you see on the board before you make a move. You need to stop, think, plan, and then make your move.

Chetski explained that we were training the students to notice the position of the chess pieces so that they could think about a move or an attack to get their own piece in a better place or at least in a position that would give them an advantage. He reminded me that each student always needed to watch where his King and Queen were, especially if the Queen was off the board. They needed to think about escape squares and how they could finally arrive at checkmate, leaving the opponent no escape. Sometimes they could force their opponent to make a move that worked to *their* advantage and not their opponent's.

As Chetski was explaining it all to me, it reminded me of my dad and my Grampy, and if I had put a bag over Chetski's head he could have been either one of them. There was a lot that I did automatically in chess, but I never really thought about any of it. Chetski ended by telling me that I needed to be really excited about getting someone else excited about a game that he hoped I thought was very, very exciting! Then he started joking around and said, "Are you cool with all this, Harry? I hope you get my rap," and we both started laughing.

When the students arrived, we spent most of that first lesson getting them set up with partners. Chetski went into this whole thing about rules and being considerate about the others in the room. I could tell that this was his thing and he was really good at making it someone else's, too. The little kids were pretty funny and some of them had what Grampy would call "motorized bodies" and mouths that were on "automatic pilot" because they just couldn't sit still or stop talking. Chetski was very enthusiastic and was sure that anyone could learn the game of chess if they really worked hard at it and concentrated.

Once we got all the beginners set up, Chetski sent me into the room with the more experienced players, asking me to sort of hang around the games and give the players some support. At first I felt really uncomfortable. Whoa man! Who is he kidding! Some of these students were a lot older and they were very good. Then a few of them started to ask me questions and I shared some of my own strategies. One of them remembered the match I had played with Dawn and he said he had even watched it on the Internet. How cool!

After everyone left, Chetski set up a board for us, but he set it up as if we were in a championship match and made the position really hard. After almost two hours I finally called checkmate. I took one of the strategies that Dawn had used on her opponent in the third round of the tournament. Chetski just sat there looking really amazed, wondering how I ever pulled it off. Finally, I explained it to him and it made all the sense in the world.

When I got home, I told Grampy all about my day and how much I enjoyed working with Chetski and watching the younger kids get into the game. Then I told him how awesome it felt to be recognized by some of the better players and to walk around and help them with their strategies. My summer was off to a better start than I had thought.

A few days later, I went to my first summer league hockey practice. It felt strange to gear up for hockey again after being away from the game for almost eight months. The first practice didn't seem very challenging and I kind of didn't like it at all. Before I went back I thought I would be afraid to play aggressively, but instead, I was bored and impatient. I was wondering if I had made a good decision. Our coach, Mr. K., went so slowly through that first practice that I felt as if I was playing ice hockey in slow motion. On the way home, I told my dad that I thought it was going to be a big waste of my time. I was really pretty worked up about it, but my dad stayed calm. I decided to call Hank and see if he wanted to hang out while I walked Zeus.

After about two weeks, Mr. K. decided to organize a game. He put third graders with fifth graders. You should have seen how fast these kids moved on the ice. They knew how to take the puck and wham, they scored two goals in the first five minutes. My wind was not half as good as theirs and neither were my feet. These kids were g-o-o-d! Age really didn't seem to matter at all. By the end of the practice I was feeling really foggy and pretty defeated. I almost wanted to give up. The coach sent the team into the locker room and asked me to hold back so he could talk to me.

In the beginning I was only half listening to what he was saying. But the more I listened the more Coach K. was making sense.

"Harry, I have a feeling that you wish that you had never come back to hockey, but here's the deal, Harry," he began. "You're trying too hard. You're trying to do too much with the puck too soon and you're losing your concentration. After two to three passes the shot should open up, but you need to focus on those passes and have a plan. Your speed will increase once you come up with a plan and stay focused. A big piece of this is confidence and feeling like you can do it. Be patient, plan, attack, and execute. You need to take charge and stop being so hard on yourself. Just tell yourself that you belong out there just as much as the other kids. Enjoy the game. We need players like you so that other players understand it is possible to get back out on the ice after an injury. You're a strong player, Harry. Remember that."

At the next practice, I had a whole new feeling about the league and my game. I couldn't wait to get out on the ice and play. Coach K. knew what he was doing and the other players on the team were really good guys. It had nothing to do with age. I wasn't even nervous about hitting the boards anymore. Looking back, I finally knew what I had done wrong the night I hit them: I had lost my concentration, the worst thing a player can do in any game.

After four practices, Coach K. brought a new kid onto the team. His name was Sam and he ended up with the locker right next to mine. When he started undressing to get into his gear, I took a double. He was wearing a back brace that looked kind of like Dawn's. One of the other players looked over and yelled, "What's with the body cage?" I remembered Dawn telling me about some of the comments that kids had made to her.

"Yo! Let a guy get dressed, will ya!" I snapped back.

Sam looked over at me and I could tell he was feelin' pretty ugly about it all.

"Just ignore them, Sam," I said. "My friend Dawn had to wear one of those braces. I keep worrying that they might put me in one someday, too."

"You have scoliosis? Well, your scoliosis must be doing better than mine," Sam snapped back in a disgusted tone. "One doctor says I need to wear a brace and another one says, don't bother, just have the operation and be done with it. My parents aren't really sure what to do. For now, I have to keep wearing the brace, except when I play sports. I will probably need surgery within the next year, but nobody is letting me in on what's going on so it's just one big secret. Anyway, Harry, that's what you said your name is. Harry. Right? I better get out on the ice. I'm very lucky this league let me in. My own league made this big deal about my brace and it was such a mess that my dad got me in here."

"No way, Sam," I said. "I didn't want to be here either, but I like Coach K. a lot and the kids on this team are awesome. I made the mistake of thinking that fifth graders shouldn't play with third graders. Was I ever wrong!"

When Sam and I got out on the ice, Coach K. seemed pretty happy that we had met and were already talking. I didn't tell him what went on in the locker room and besides, I was hoping it wouldn't happen again. This was a "between the guys" thing and as long as everyone was safe, it was going to be okay.

Out on the ice, Sam was as rusty as I was when I first started and I could see that it was really getting to him. His wind was really bad and he was panting as he went across the ice. He was so busy trying to do everything all at once that he reminded me of myself at my first practice. The only difference was that Sam let it all hang out. He was having a conversation with himself about how poorly he was doing and he just kept dissing and dissing. He seemed to have all the answers. No one dared say a word to him, not even Coach K., who just let him go and get it all out. Sam sure had attitude.

Meanwhile, each time we played I tried to pass to Sam as much as I could. Finally, I got so annoyed at him for not taking the passes that I yelled out, "Sam, try and think about where we're going with the puck."

He looked over at me with this puzzled look on his face and then yelled back, "Sweet, Harry. Let's show these peewees how the big guys play."

The younger kids on the team weren't gonna stand for that too long and pretty soon we had one heck of a game going.

Our practices were pretty awesome after Sam arrived and I looked forward to them all week long. We had definitely become a team, and when Sam came in the locker room the younger guys would joke around and say things like, "Here comes Sam in his armor." Sam would just laugh and call them "short legs" or something like that but not in a mean way at all.

As for Sam and me, we got to be pretty good friends. I found out that he lived in Cambridge, across the Charles River from Boston. His parents were divorced and so he really lived in two places. He seemed okay with the divorce, but not so okay with the living in two places. It was very confusing for him and sometimes he said that he just wanted to stay in one place. I guess when grownups get divorced nobody ever asks the kids what they want. Sam had an older sister who was in high school. She sometimes brought him to practice because she had her driver's license. It kind of made me miss Consuela being around. I liked his sister and a few times she ended up giving me a ride home.

Eventually I found out that Sam and I went to the same hospital for our scoliosis, but to different doctors. Sam learned that he had scoliosis when he was in first grade, but his curve had become worse. He asked me what kind of scoliosis I had and for a minute I couldn't even remember. So I asked him back what kind he had and he said it was called juvenile idiopathic. As soon as he used the idiopathic word I knew that it was the same word that Dr. Roberts had used with me. What I was unsure of was the juvenile part. Then Sam asked me when I had found out I had scoliosis. When I told him, he said that I only had the idiopathic part and not the juvenile stuff. Sounded pretty confusing to me, but I didn't want to tell Sam that. And besides, he's not a doctor so he might not be right.

The summer was flying by. In late July, Tommy came into Boston and spent the weekend with me. He was kind of disappointed that Herbie was visiting relatives in North Carolina, but Hank came over and we hung out and played basketball and then went over to the Boy's Club. Tommy always kept us laughing, but sometimes Hank would look over and just roll his eyes and I knew that Tommy had scored again! We really had a great time and I think Grampy would have let Tommy move in if someone made the offer.

When Tommy's mom and dad came to pick him up, they asked me if I could come out to their house for a weekend. This was something I hadn't done before and I kind of wanted to, but I wasn't sure what the weekend would be like. Whenever I spent time with Tommy, Jack was there, too. This would be different. Before I could answer, my parents said that they thought I would enjoy that and that we would look at our schedule and give Tommy's parents a call. I was kind of annoyed that my parents had answered for me, but I guess I would have said yes for myself.

Chapter Nine

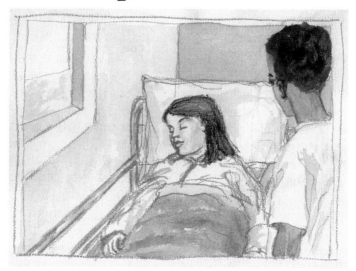

I went to see Dawn that week in the hospital, but she ended up just wanting to sleep, so my mom said we'd wait and visit with her once she got home and was doing better. Dawn e-mailed me with the medical update on her back once she was home so I got all the gory details firsthand, except they really weren't very gory at all. Finally, my mom called Dawn's mother and asked if we could go over for a visit. Dawn was very excited that we were coming. She made me promise to bring my magnetic chessboard. I was really looking forward to the visit, especially since I had never really spent any time at her house before.

Dawn lived in an area near Boston called the South Shore and you could kind of smell the ocean as you drove into her town. Our whole family piled into the car for the visit. Even Grampy got to go and I think he was more excited than I was. He had gotten to know Dawn and her family from the chess tournament in Colorado. Our families had spent a lot of time together during that weekend. Now it felt like we were old friends.

When we pulled into Dawn's driveway, her dog, Rufus, met us at the door. I kind of wished that we had brought Zeus, but he wasn't always great with other dogs. Mom said he always stirred them up. Dawn was standing right behind Rufus and she looked great. I wouldn't have known she had just had surgery unless someone told me.

While the adults hung out, Dawn and I went into the back-yard and played chess while her brother, Paul, watched. I was amazed at how comfortable Dawn looked and felt. She said that she could finally wear her own size clothes. I had never noticed that her other clothes looked big but I decided not to tell Dawn that. Our chess game went on and on so Dawn and I didn't get to talk very much. I think she was getting even for my last win. Finally, after sitting there with nothing moving for almost thirty minutes, she played a brilliant combination and won the game. I could tell she was very proud of herself. It was definitely payback time for Colorado.

After the game, Dawn gave me a tour of her house and I was amazed at the number of chess trophies she had. There was something to do with chess in almost every room. We talked a little about the game and she told me that the Kings of K–12 was the first time she had lost a big tournament, ever. It made me feel really bad until Dawn started laughing and said, "Harry, don't feel bad. It's not over yet. I'm just going to work harder at beating you the next time." Then we both started laughing together.

I was really curious about Dawn's surgery since I still didn't know a lot about scoliosis and I was worried that I might need an operation someday myself. She told me that they had hoped to wait longer before operating, but that she had a very serious curve and the doctors felt it was time.

"What's a serious curve?" I asked, feeling kind of stupid about all this scoliosis stuff. Dawn never really looked like any-thing serious was wrong with her.

"Well, Harry, this is what happened," Dawn began. "When I was in second grade, I went to my pediatrician for a checkup and he had me do this bending thing. I got the feeling he was interested in my back. Finally, he told my mother that he thought my back wasn't straight. I don't remember the whole conversation, but I do know that I wasn't feeling so great about it all, especially when he said that he wanted me to see another doctor and have all this back stuff checked out."

"Dawn, that's what a doctor told my parents, too," I said, "except it wasn't my pediatrician, it was the doctor in the hospital who took care of me after my hockey injury."

"Well, Harry, I had to see the back doctor, an orthopedist, because my back wouldn't stop curving. They told me it was almost 55 degrees curved before my surgery. They said it would be safer for me to have the surgery sooner rather than later. The doctor said I had something called a 'progressive curve.' If you want, Harry, I can show you my before-and-after spine pictures. They gave them to us at the hospital."

Just as Dawn said that I looked up and her mother was standing in the doorway.

"I'll let Dawn show you her pictures if your mom thinks it's okay, Harry. In fact, your mom can explain them since she's a nurse and knows a lot more about these things than we do."

"What's this about back pictures?" My mom came in with kind of a funny look on her face.

While Dawn's mom was explaining it all to my mom, Paul went and got the pictures and before I knew it we were all looking at them and having this big talk about scoliosis. Dawn's back really did look much better and it helped me a lot since scoliosis is something that none of the kids ever talk about. It's like this big secret or something. Sam had spoken about it a little, but Dawn had a better way of helping me to understand it all. Sam was kind of angry so he made me a little nervous.

After we ate, I told Dawn about Sam and how they had teased him in the locker room because he had a brace. She told me that sometimes the kids had given her funny looks and a few times some of the kids had asked her questions about her brace, but no one had ever made her feel bad about it. She said that after a while she just wanted the surgery over with. Then she said that her mom also had scoliosis and because no one ever noticed her mom's, they didn't watch it carefully like they did Dawn's. Fortunately, her mom's scoliosis was very slight.

I still didn't completely understand all this stuff. I was also getting a little worried about my own back. It looked okay to me, but Dr. Roberts said that this could change. Since Consuela had been lucky, I was hoping I would be, too. And I have to admit that I never looked at Dawn's back before the surgery because she was always in the brace. People just don't go around checking out backs.

Dawn laughed when I told her that and then said, "It's all behind me now! Get it?"

Dawn can be very funny, even though everyone thinks she's this really serious, brainy girl.

When it was time to go home, I think my parents said good-bye at least five times before they actually said the "real good-bye." They set a time for when Dawn and her family could come to Boston and visit us. It was still hot out and we only have air-conditioning in our bedrooms so they decided on early fall, when the weather would be cooler.

The weekend was over before I knew it and it was time to go to chess and hockey practice. I had finally gotten into a routine and it was working pretty well.

Hank and I got together most evenings, which was great, and Herbie wrote to us a lot from North Carolina. According to Herbie, everything in North Carolina seemed to be mad-good, mad-bad, or mad-loud. Leave it to Herbie to come up with a new way of saying something. Hank and I cracked up about it whenever we saw each other and sometimes we would compare letters. They were exactly the same except Herbie had addressed mine "Dear Harry" and Hank's "Dear Hank."

I also hung out a little with Sam. The first place Sam and I went to was his neighborhood ice cream store in Cambridge. It was huge compared to the one we went to in Boston. It seemed kind of odd that Cambridge was a smaller city than Boston but had a much bigger ice cream store.

My weekend with Tommy had come and gone and I had had an awesome time with him, too. His mom and dad were a lot of fun and the first thing we did was make homemade ice cream in his backyard. This definitely was my ice cream summer. It seemed like every minute there was something new to see in his house or yard. Tommy always made it seem like his house was a drag, but it was really fun. I think the big problem was that it was way out of town and he didn't have any kids his age nearby. His mom and dad told me nearly every hour how happy they were that I had come. Tommy said that I was his first friend ever to spend the night.

That was hard to believe, but when I thought about it more, I could understand. Tommy was a really cool kid but as Grampy explained, Tommy didn't think he was very cool. Grampy said that because of this he sometimes made bad choices. I was happy that he was making some better ones.

Chapter Ten

S ummer had really flown. It was hard to believe that there were only three weeks left before school started up. I was all done with my chess tutoring and had played in a lot of tournaments, all of which Dawn had won. She was really on a roll, but the important thing for me to keep in mind was that I knew I was also very good. Each time she won, I learned something new about the game.

My hockey league turned out to be awesome and the coach had asked both Sam and me if we would consider playing in the fall in our own leagues. Sam had to wait and see what his doctor said, and I knew for sure that I really wanted to be back on my local team. I didn't even think about the boards anymore and I had a very different feeling about younger players. Coach K. made all of us feel like winners and on the night of our last practice, he made a speech that would have made any hockey player feel like he was "standing tall." Although I really liked Coach Miller, I would miss Coach K. and all the kids I had met on his team.

The weekend after practice ended it was time for the big picnic at Walden Pond. Jack had just gotten home from camp and this was the first time I would get to see him since June. I was unbelievably excited and part of me just wanted to visit with him alone. I know that sounds kind of selfish but he's one of my best friends in the whole world.

We were all so excited to be together again that the whole beach heard us. Everybody was hugging and shaking hands. It was a sweet, sunny, hot day and our mothers had brought all the fixin's for one heck of a picnic and barbecue. Of course, Tommy started with dessert and managed to sneak a few of my mother's double fudge brownies before we went off on a hike with our dads. I knew my mother saw him take them and I was proud of her for not saying anything. Tommy was definitely another Herbie.

We hiked, ate, flew kites, and Tommy even got a swimming lesson from Jack's dad. It was just an awesome day and I didn't want it to ever end. Tommy, Jack, and I sat under some trees and talked for what seemed like hours. I was so excited to tell Jack more about Zeus. Even though I had written a letter to him right after we got Zeus, telling someone in person was much better. Each time I told a Zeus story, Tommy would yell out, "Yeah, yeah, that's what he does Jack!" Then Jack would give Tommy that same look he used to give in school and we busted up laughing.

Just before we packed up to leave, Tommy asked Jack and me if we were scared about starting middle school. I hadn't really given it much thought except that I was excited to be in the same school as my friend Jeb. Jack looked confused by Tommy's question, but didn't say much. Then I started to think about what Grampy had said about how new things were hard for Tommy and I knew he was worried that we might all be placed in different classes. It would be really hard if Jack and Tommy and I split up.

"Tommy, what are you the most worried about?" I asked.

"Well, Harry. What if we get put in classes with other kids and we aren't together anymore? What if you and Jack get to be together and they put me in another room?"

"Tommy, whatever happens we will still be really good friends and we will see each other at recess and lunch," I answered. "We might all end up in different classes, Tommy, but getting all upset about it isn't going to help. Let's just wait and see."

"But Harry, what if none of the kids in my class wants to be my friend?"

I could tell that Tommy was really worried and I was a little nervous myself, but not about friends, just about being in a new school and a new room. But now, listening to Tommy, I was starting to get kind of anxious.

Then Jack started, "What if, what if? We'll just have to wait and see where we go because we can't do anything about it now, can we?"

Jack sounded exactly like Dawn. Just as I was about to agree with Jack but maybe say it a little differently so Tommy would feel better, our parents gave the last call for home. I

could see by the look on Tommy's face that he had been thinking about this school stuff for a while.

After we got home, Sam called. I had phoned him a few
days earlier and asked if he wanted to come over and spend
the night the following week. Mom had a day off in the middle
of the week and I had promised Sam an overnight before
school started.

I spent the next few days hanging out with Zeus and
Grampy and playing basketball with Hank. Herbie would be
home the same day that Sam was coming over, so I was kind
of hoping that Sam could meet my neighborhood friends. I
couldn't wait to hear how Sam's doctor's appointment had
gone and if he was going to be able to play hockey in the fall.
Sam said that this was going to be important because his
doctor would explain what needed to be done for his back.

Sam's father dropped him off early in the morning on his
way to work. Mom had made my favorite breakfast, griddlecakes and sausage, and Sam looked as if he had never had
such a great breakfast before in his whole life. He must have
told my mom the pancakes were "Mmmm-good" at least ten
times. Grampy told Sam it sounded like a new pancake song!

While I showered, Sam hung out with Zeus and Grampy,
and when I came out of my room, Grampy was teaching Sam
how to play chess. It took me almost an hour to drag Sam
away from Grampy and the chessboard.

Sam loved the city and we explored my neighborhood and
even met Mr. Peace and Old Blue as we were winding down
the tour. Sam told me that when he was really little, he and his
parents had lived in South Boston and that the house he and
his parents had lived in is now a small restaurant. I said that
sometimes Grampy points out restaurants in our area and
says they used to be so-and-so's house. I guess neighborhoods change. Grampy says that over time everything
changes and sometimes it's a good thing and sometimes it's
not such a good thing.

Just as Sam and I were running up the front steps to my
house, I heard Herbie and Hank calling me. I was so excited to

see Herbie that I slammed the door shut on Zeus, who was trying very hard to sneak out.

"Herbie, hey man, you're home! I was hoping today would be the day! Come on up and met my friend Sam!"

Herbie took three giant steps and he was at the door. I couldn't believe how much taller he looked.

"Hey brother, whasssss up? What's shakin' man?" yelled Herbie as he followed me up the steps toward Sam.

Herbie was just the same, and before I could answer he slapped me five, introduced himself to Sam, and had pushed his way into our front door and was on the floor wrestling with Zeus. My mother came out to see who was causing all the noise.

"Herbie! Great to see you," my mom said. "You look wonderful and I guess all that family down south didn't change you one bit. You're still shaking up this house, now, aren't you?"

"Hi, Mrs. Jones. I've been thinkin' about your cookin' all summer," laughed Herbie.

"I bet you say that to all the mothers, Herbie, but if you come on back I think I can find something special for you," answered my mom as she walked back to the kitchen.

"You know I'll be there," Herbie called after her. "You know how my stomach is attracted to your food."

After Herbie and Hank met Sam, Herbie headed for the kitchen while Hank, Sam, and I played some computer games. Sam was really awesome and he told Hank and me that he spent most evenings on his computer. I was kind of wishing that I could do the same, but man do my parents have rules. There are rules in my house for just about everything. There are even summertime rules.

When Herbie got done eating everything that wasn't nailed down, he wandered back into the family room to see what we were up to. As soon as he got a better view of Sam, he wore that very scary "Herbie look" and I just knew he was about ready to fire off a bunch of questions to Sam about his back brace. Before he got started, I decided to help Sam out or maybe even give him some support.

"Sam, Herbie's my friend who now says that everything is 'mad-good' or 'mad-bad.' Remember I was telling you about all the crazy letters he sent to Hank and me?"

Sam gave me this blank look as if to say, "What are you talkin' about?"

"And Herbie, I need to warn Sam that you are probably gonna ask him a bunch of questions about his back brace, but I need you to know that it's a lot like the one that my chess friend, Dawn, wore and I don't think Sam really wants to talk about it. Do you get my drift, Herbie?"

I hardly got the last few words out of my mouth when Sam called out, "You got that right, Harry. I do not want to talk about this brace, Herbie, so just don't even waste your time asking!"

Herbie got the message loud and clear, even though you could tell he had a few questions that were still bothering him. For the rest of the afternoon we all just hung out and listened to Herbie tell stories about his cousins in North Carolina and how hot it was down there. And by hot, I don't mean how cool it was to be there and not up here. Herbie always made it sound like it was this big deal having to spend his summer down south, but Hank and I knew that Herbie loved going. He was really close to his family and most of his relatives lived in the South, so it was like a reunion when he got down there. He was like the "king" cousin from the North and he loved all the attention. Grampy said that's why his parents sent him, because at home he's the youngest of four boys and hardly has much of a say in things.

Just before dinner we went over to play some hoops in the park. Sam took his brace off for about an hour. He was allowed to choose when he wanted his brace-free time. Sam was really competitive, and what started out as just throwing hoops in a basket became a two-against-two game. Hank and I were on one team and Sam and Herbie were on the other. We were having such a big time out there that even Herbie's older brother and some of his friends cleared the courts for us. We really had a great time and I could tell that Sam was excited about being out of the brace. He and Herbie made quite a team and the two of them never stopped talking the whole time they were playing. Hank and I had the quieter side and we really had to holler to get our voices heard.

The hour went by really fast and before we knew it, my dad was standing on the sidelines telling us that it was time to call it a game and come on home. My mother had phoned Herbie's and Hank's parents and cleared the way for them to join us for dinner. We were barbecuing and I think my dad ended up cooking hamburgers for the better part of an hour, knowing that four hungry basketball players would be ready for a good meal. My mom made my grandmother's baked bean recipe and a great salad using lettuce from Grampy's victory garden up the street. Victory gardens are neat. In the city they let people have some open space for small gardens and they call them victory gardens. Grampy has had one for thirty years and in this very small space he can grow every-thing from lettuce to pumpkins. Sometimes, in the late spring, I go and help him plant. It is an awesome way to live in the city and still have a garden. And it sure makes for a great salad.

Dinner was very noisy and a lot of fun, too. I saw my parents giving each other that parent look they exchange when the kids are out of control. I think you probably know what I mean. For me, it was "mad-good" to have Sam meet Herbie and Hank, and really great to have Herbie home.

My mother's clue that it was time for quiet was to announce that showers were happening right after dinner. We were all very smelly from shooting hoops. As soon as she mentioned showers, Herbie and Hank checked out and said good-bye. I was ready to have some downtime with Sam anyway, although I think Sam was kind of sad that they were leaving. His life at home was similar to Tommy's, very quiet, and I think Sam was alone a lot, just like Tommy.

After we each took a shower, Sam asked if we could play some chess. I was surprised but also kind of excited. I had gotten to be a good chess teacher and I enjoyed showing kids how to play the game. I knew that my Grampy had already given Sam some pointers so I decided to set up a game and give him some help as we played. I was amazed at how many of the basics he remembered. He knew the names of all the chess pieces, and he remembered how they moved. Still, he was pretty easy to beat, but I kind of let the game drag out a while so he would learn more about strategies. Then I told him about how Tommy, Jack, and I had started a chess club at our elementary school. That kind of made me sad since I would soon be moving on to middle school. I was beginning to understand why Tommy was feeling worried about a new school. Maybe I was a little worried myself.

Sam and I were so tired after our chess game that I don't even remember saying good night to him. He ended up sleeping until almost ten o'clock the next morning and I could tell that he loved being able to stay in one place for a while. He told me that even before his parents got divorced they each worked, so he went to a lot of camps in the summer. Even though both my parents worked, I was lucky to have my Grampy so I could sleep late and stay home and just hang out.

It wasn't that hot out so Sam and I decided to gear up and have a street hockey game on one of the side streets near my house. It was a dead-end street so there were never very many cars. I called Herbie and even though he said he hated playing hockey, he agreed to join us. Hank was busy so one of Herbie's brothers came out, too. Once we got started, a few other kids from around the neighborhood joined in. Sam was definitely out of his brace more than an hour, but he said it was okay since he was about to stop wearing it. He explained that he hadn't been very good about keeping up the schedule and then went into more detail.

"Harry, my curve has been progressing despite my brace so my doctor is talking more and more about the possibility of surgery," said Sam.

Before long, Grampy showed up and got Sam's attention by pointing to his wrist. Sam got the message and we called it a game so he could get his brace back on. We were all getting really hot and tired, anyway.

Grampy treated us to pizza for lunch and made us promise to bring back two pieces for him. Herbie and his brother went on home since they had to do their chores. I had a few of my own, but my parents said while Sam was visiting they would help out.

When we got home, Sam and I just hung out, talked, and played with my computer. His mom came to pick him up at about five-thirty. Sam's mom was really nice and told me that

Sam enjoyed having me as his friend. She said that his summer got a lot better once we hooked up. I told her that it was the same for me and I could see that Sam was really happy about that.

"Harry, are you going back to your old hockey league or are you staying with your summer league coach?" she asked.

I was surprised at her question.

"I don't know, Mrs. Stevens. I haven't even thought about that."

"Well, Harry, you know Sam is not happy with his old league because they are concerned about his scoliosis," said Sam's mom. "As his doctor has said, many people do not understand that scoliosis has no effect on Sam's ability to do what everyone else does. His league is worried about an injury, even though Sam's doctor wrote a note and said he could play. We are now trying to find another league for him to join."

My dad, who was listening, told Sam's mom about Coach Miller. He even offered to give Coach Miller a call and tell him about Sam. Sam's mom appreciated the help, but Sam looked a little embarrassed. He had told me about all the trouble he had with his hockey league and how bad he felt about it. He really loved his old coach, but I guess the league that he played in made the rules and they didn't seem to know very much about scoliosis. I was kind of excited that Sam might be on my team again, but my dad said it was up to Coach Miller and our local league. If it turned out that Sam was too old for Coach Miller's team, my dad said that there was another team that he might be able to join. Sam slapped me five when he left. We had really enjoyed a great time together.

Chapter Eleven

I spent most of the next week getting ready to go back to school. I had been given a summer reading list and I needed to finish the last book. Both my parents were on vacation so we took a lot of day trips to different places in the area including my first visit to the John F. Kennedy Library here in Boston.

The library and exhibits were unlike anything I had ever seen before. They even had President Kennedy's voice talking to us and that was very creepy since he isn't alive anymore. It made my parents and my Grampy get all teary. When I saw the pictures of President Kennedy with his family it kind of made me sad, too. Then we went into a special room and watched the video that had Dr. Martin Luther King making his "I have a dream" speech. My parents and my Grampy got even more weepy, and I was thinking that this wasn't such a great field trip. My Grampy took my hand and held it really tight and whispered in my ear that times like this help all of us to

remember the importance of peace and caring about everyone in the world, not just caring about yourself. It made me
listen harder to what Dr. King was saying and when I looked
into his eyes I could see how he was just like my Grampy. Mrs.
Lamont would say that Dr. King had eyes that talked, even if
you weren't listening to his words. His eyes looked so deep
and caring and it made me sad, because he was "good people"
and he was gone.

On the way home my parents talked about how important it
is to understand history and the things that have happened in
our country. In school we called it Social Studies, but I think
it's the same thing. I had heard Mom and Dad say stuff like
that before, but now I understood better what they meant.
Grampy kept saying that President Kennedy, his brother,
Senator Robert Kennedy, and Dr. Martin Luther King were all
people who cared about how we could all live together in
peace. Dr. King was a great man who helped the world understand that all people should have the opportunity to live in
freedom. Even though I was kind of young to get all that, I
think I knew why they wanted me to hear his speech.

On another day we decided to go to the beach and I called
Jack to see if he could join us. His father drove him into
Boston the day before we went so that we could have an
overnight. After dinner, Jack and I hung out with Herbie and
Hank. They had gotten to know Jack pretty well and he was
like part of the "hood" now. He had an amazing memory. I
couldn't believe that Jack remembered that one of Herbie's
brothers was always reading SpongeBob comic and puzzle
books. Jack also remembered all the annoying stuff that
Herbie's brothers did. I thought that was weird, but Herbie
said that when you meet a famous person you remember
every little detail about them.

The next day my parents, Jack, and I went to the beach.
Grampy stayed home with Zeus. I kind of wanted to bring
Zeus with us, but dogs were not allowed on the beach and
my dad said he might end up with sand fleas. Not my dad,
Zeus!

Chapter Eleven

We spent the whole day next to the water, and Jack and I built this huge sand fort. It was so cool. All the little kids near us just stood and watched this amazing fort going up. One little boy kept asking, "What ya gonna make now?" Jack said he sounded like a tape recording because he said it over and over.

"Harry, why does he keep asking us the same thing?" Jack whispered to me kind of annoyed.

"Heck, I don't know, Jack. I think it's just a little kid thing. Just smile at him and tell him to keep watching 'cause we want to surprise him!" I answered.

Jack called out to the little boy and then there was this long pause, almost too long, and I knew Jack was trying to figure out what he wanted to say to the little guy. Finally Jack blurted it out, which was not like Jack at all.

"Hey little guy, ya know what? What we're building next is a big secret and if you watch very carefully and very quietly, you will be the first to know the secret."

The little boy got all excited and after that all he did was watch us. In fact, he just sat there and stared at us for the longest time. Finally, his mom came over and said it was time for him to leave. As she scooped up the kicking and screaming child, Jack and I just kind of smiled at each other. Maybe we should have told his mom our secret to keeping the little guy quiet!

When the sun started to get closer and closer to land, the tide came in and filled our fort with water, which was kind of a bummer since we had worked on it most of the day. My parents had brought a Frisbee so we all played a game. We even got my mom to jump around and play. Once the mosquitoes came out, the game ended pretty quickly. No matter how fast you run around, the mosquitoes seem to be able to fly faster than you can run. They're like tiny biting jets!

We didn't get home until about eight-thirty. My mom called Jack's parents on her cell phone and asked if he could spend a second night. There was going to be an open house at our new middle school the next day. My mom offered to bring us both out there. Jack's mom said that we could meet at their house and all go on the tour together. I had almost forgotten all about it and I was really glad that Jack and I would be visiting at the same time. I kind of wished that we had called Tommy so that he could come with us, but it was really last minute. When I mentioned it to Jack, he said that his mom had called Tommy's house and there was no answer.

Jack and I had planned on playing a chess game before we went to bed, but we were so tired that we ended up just "hitting the sack." When we got into bed, we started talking about school and whether or not we would be in the same class. I tried to act cool about it, kind of like it didn't matter.

At first Jack was the same and then he said, " I never really cared who was in my class before, Harry, but now I really hope we end up together. I'm sure I'll do fine if you're not in my class, but we like the same things and we can even read each other's minds, if you know what I mean. I never really hung out with anybody as much as I hang out with you. You've even got me thinking about playing soccer this fall."

"Wow, Jack, that is so awesome because I may go back to hockey. We can go to each others' games!" I was very excited.

It was major for Jack to try soccer again. It was also major for him to talk about his feelings since he never did that kind of stuff.

"It's not for sure, Harry, but I think I'll play soccer. I'm just kind of tossing it around in my mind," said Jack.

I could tell that he really wanted to play, but he was just a little nervous about who his coach was going to be. The last coach yelled and screamed at Jack and when the coach wasn't putting Jack down, his son was. I'm sure glad that I never had a coach like that.

I was so excited thinking about Jack trying soccer again that I forgot all about school. I went from being wiped out from the sun and a little worried about starting at the middle school to being wide awake thinking about sports, chess, and all sorts of fun stuff.

"Herbie, wait a minute now, Harry is still asleep. He only has a few more days left to sleep late so I don't want to wake him up. Jack spent another night so I don't want you waking up either of them. I promise to have Harry call you when he finally wakes up."

I could hear my mom talking to Herbie in the background as I rolled over looking for my pillow and the clock. My pillow had landed in Jack's face, but he looked totally out of it. He was sound asleep and it looked as if someone had thrown everything on top of him. He was definitely a "sheet wrestler," at least that's what it looked like to me.

I tried to slide out of bed quietly so that I wouldn't wake Jack. All of a sudden my pillow came flying up in the air and I heard this strange sound, like an engine warming up. Jack never went right into a laugh; he worked up to one! I thought about calling out to Herbie, who was still begging my mother to go in and wake us up. But I decided that I didn't have the energy to move into "high Herbie gear."

By the time Jack and I were washed and dressed, we could smell bacon coming from the kitchen. Even though it smelled really good, I warned Jack that my mother was a nurse and would definitely explain that it was not a healthy food and that she only cooked it because my dad bought it and nobody should waste food. Even though my mom never put it on her own plate, we always saw her sneaking at least one piece into her mouth while she was cooking.

While Jack and I finished our breakfast, my dad and Grampy started up a game of chess. Grampy would play chess all day if he could and I think the same is probably true of my dad. Grampy always did all these eye tricks to try to distract my dad from the piece that Grampy was really eyeing, but my dad was now onto what was going on. So was I because Grampy had explained to me why he did the eye stuff and since I got so good at chess, I think my Grampy kind of wishes he had kept his tricks a secret.

I was beginning to get a little nervous about middle school and this whole thing about having to start out at a new school again. I had ended at Mercier on such a high that I knew leaving all that behind and going to a new school might not feel as good. Look how many years it took for me to feel connected to Mercier.

My dad was working on some business stuff on his computer so my mom and Jack's mom decided we'd meet at Jack's house, have a quick lunch, and then go on the tour. No one *had* to go on the tour, but it was a way to get to know where everything was before the first day of school. The Read Middle School was huge compared to Mercier. Dawn told me in an e-mail that her school did the same thing.

"It beats going to a new school and not knowing where anything is," she wrote.

In the car on the way out, Jack and I talked about what it would really be like at Read. Yo! It was less than a week away. I told him that even though I didn't think I would be nervous, I was starting to feel a little uncomfortable about it all. Tommy was right, this might not be so easy because we would be the lowest class and there would be lots of new kids. I began to notice that Jack was getting kind of quiet in the car and he was giving me very short answers. I got the feeling that he was more anxious than he was saying. In a way, I was lucky because I knew a lot of the Boston kids from the bus so I already had a little connection. My friend Jeb was in the sixth grade and he seemed to be pretty hot on school. He also said there were lots of clubs and sports things going on. There was even a chess club and I thought that was very, very cool.

We had a great time at Jack's and Mrs. James made us a lunch that didn't look like mystery food. It was something my own mom would have made.

After lunch, I played with Jack's rabbit. This was one lucky rabbit; it went anywhere it wanted in Jack's house. It had this litter box in the back hall so no one ever had to walk it. How cool is that to have a rabbit loose around your house?

Pretty soon it was time to go. I kind of wanted to spend more time at Jack's, but I knew we needed to do this. At least our mothers thought we did. We piled into Jack's car and off we went. And I have to admit, I really was a little nervous.

The Read Middle School was very large compared to our Mercier Elementary. We checked in at the office and ahead of us was the longest hallway I had ever seen. On one side was the auditorium, which looked bigger than the Boy's Club basketball courts, and on the other side of the hall was this huge cafeteria, with juice machines and a salad bar sign that looked like something you'd see in a restaurant. A man came out and announced that he was Mr. Orelup, the fifth-grade guidance counselor, and he would be taking us on the tour along with Mrs. MacDonald, who was one of the fifth-grade classroom teachers. They both seemed pretty upbeat and they made the tour fun. They each told us stories about other kids who had made the change from one building to the other and some of the things they had written down about why they liked middle school. Many of the comments were really funny, like being able to vote on lunch once a month or not having your mother or father walk you to your classroom door, and the best was not having to give Valentines to girls anymore. They also wrote about what they missed, like no more candy when they got help with phonics, no more rabbits jumping and brushing on their pant legs in kindergarten, and no more puppet shows with the guidance counselor. Hearing their stories helped me to relax a little bit, even though Jack said they were corny.

The tour lasted about an hour and at the end the assistant principal came out and greeted us. She had been in a meeting and couldn't come and greet us all until the end of the tour. She reminded me a little of Mrs. Starck from Mercier. She came right over to Jack and me and started talking to us about chess. She said she recognized us from our picture in the local paper and said that she had already met Tommy. Then she went around and shook hands with each student and their parents. I wanted to ask her if I could be in Jack and Tommy's class, but I decided it might not be a good idea. But what a mind reader she was.

She ended by saying, "I'm sure each one of you has at least one friend that you would like to have in your class and hopefully that will happen. We try very hard to make that possible and we do a pretty good job of it. I look forward to seeing all of you next week. You should receive your letters with your class placement either today or tomorrow. If you are going out of town, they will be posted in several areas of the building the first week of school and they will also be online. A copy of the school website is at the bottom of each letter. Welcome and I hope you have a wonderful year."

I felt much better after the tour. We got back to Jack's house and had a quick glass of lemonade. The mail was there when we arrived and Jack found the middle school letter addressed to his parents. Just as he was about to open it, his mom took it away and said that he had to wait since it would be rude to open it in front of me because I didn't have mine. Rude, shrude! That wasn't true at all. I thought it was ruder *not* to open it. Jack didn't look happy about it at all and I just wanted to get home to see if my letter had arrived. I usually liked to hang out at Jack's as long as I could but this day was different. Just like Jack I gulped down my lemonade and before we knew it we had said good-bye and my mom and I were on our way back to Beantown. I promised Jack that I would e-mail him as soon as I opened my letter.

Chapter Twelve

"**M**om, I can't believe this. How come Jack gets his school mail before us? This is so unfair. Why didn't the school mail my letter out a day earlier so we could all find out at the same time?" I squawked to my mom when we arrived home.

"Harry Jones, you just calm down now. I am sure your letter will come first thing tomorrow morning. I know how hard this is, but there is nothing we can do about it now," answered my mom. I could tell by the sound of her voice that she was kind of disappointed, too.

"Now, wait just one minute," called out Grampy. "I have a lot of pull in the post office. Remember, I used to work there and I got mail from all over the world. How about if I sneak into the mailroom and go through all the bags and find that darn letter?"

I knew Grampy was joking and trying to help, but I was so bummed out about not getting my letter that even Grampy couldn't make me feel better.

"Sorry, Grampy," I said. "I don't think your post office humor is going to work tonight."

Grampy walked by and gave me a pat on the shoulder. Then he picked up Zeus's leash. Even though he was trying to make it easier for me, it just wasn't going to work. I was really disappointed.

I decided to e-mail Jack and tell him the bad news, but before I got to my computer, the phone rang. It was Jack.

"Harry, you're just not going to believe this. You and I are in the same room. My mom finally let me open the letter from school. I have the list and we're both on it. The bad part is that Tommy isn't and when I called his house again there was no answer."

"Jack, that is so awesome," I shouted. "Mom, Dad! Jack and

I are in the same room this year. He's got the list and we're both on it. That is so cool. I don't even need my letter."

I could hear my parents cheering. Then I remembered Grampy.

"Jack, wait a minute, will ya?"

I ran over and yelled out my front window, "Grampy, Jack is on the phone and we're going to be in the same class."

"Jack, I'll e-mail you after dinner. Herbie is outside putting on quite a show."

"Okay, Harry. I kind of wish I could see what Herbie is up to. It's pretty quiet out here."

When I hung up with Jack, Herbie had already made his way into my house and was still giving a show as he came up the stairs. Normally, my mom will try to calm him down, but she was really digging Herbie's humor and so was my dad. When Grampy came in with Zeus, it didn't take long for him and Zeus to join in and get excited along with us. Zeus started barking and jumping up on everyone.

Herbie came pretty close to having dinner with us, but then his mother tracked him down and said he had to go home because he had never told her where he was going. My mom got on the phone and tried to help Herbie out, but he hadn't finished his chores either so it was a done deal.

I e-mailed Jack after dinner. He had already sent me an e-mail about finding Tommy's name on another class list. Tommy still didn't answer his phone. Jack and I were kind of worried. It wasn't like Tommy to just disappear. When Jack told me who was in that class, I had a feeling Tommy would be okay. He had been friends with another kid in third grade who would be with him again. Hopefully, it would work out, but I felt bad that we all didn't get to be together. I knew that Tommy would be really disappointed, too.

"Harry, hurry up or you'll miss the bus. It is almost six-fifteen," called my mom.

"Harry, did you hear your mom? You have very little time before your bus rounds the corner."

That was my dad. I felt like there was an echo coming down my back hall. Next thing you know, my Grampy would be upstairs asking me if I heard my mom and dad! It didn't take long for that nice, relaxing, summer-vacation feeling to go back to the old rushing school routine.

"Okay, okay. I'm coming," I called out from my bedroom. What I really wanted to say was, "Cool it you guys. Just cool it," but there was no room for backtalk in my house. Oh, man, if I called that out it would open up a whole other problem.

As I ran down the front steps, I could feel the dampness. It was a rainy, muggy day and my new shirt felt and probably smelled like I had been wearing it for a lot longer than fifteen minutes. Why is it that the first day of school is always so ugly? It's always really hot, really rainy, or both.

By the time I got to the last step my dad was behind me reading off the list that my mom had made up of all the things I needed. I was glad that the first day of school only came once a year.

"Dad, I can't stop now. I'm gonna miss the bus!"

"Okay, Harry. I hope you have everything you need," called out my dad.

Just when I thought I was done, my mom came racing down the steps looking for her kiss good-bye. Fortunately, I was pretty far down the sidewalk and I could hear my dad telling her that I was in middle school now and too big for kisses on the sidewalk. It sounded so funny hearing my dad say that, and I laughed all the way to the bus stop.

When I looked ahead, I could see Grampy and Zeus waiting for me. I knew Grampy had offered to walk Zeus but I figured he had taken the same route as Mr. Peace and Old Blue. Grampy had this big smile on his face and Zeus looked like he was feeling just as happy as Grampy.

"This was Zeus's idea, Harry," said Grampy. "He wanted to see you off on your big day. Middle school is special. It's one of those things people call milestones, special times that you will always remember. Don't worry, Zeus and I talked and neither of us will ask you for a kiss good-bye!" teased my Grampy.

We both started laughing and Zeus went into one of his barking fits.

"Here comes the bus. I'll just act like I'm walking the dog, Harry. You don't need me meeting and greeting you at the bus anymore. Have a great day, son."

When the bus pulled up, I could see Jeb banging on the window. I was surprised that Mr. Barrett wasn't driving. The new bus driver seemed to understand what I was thinking and called out, "Good morning, Harry Jones. I'm the new Mr. Barrett; just call me Bob. This is the middle and high school bus now. We've split the drive from Boston this year. Mr. Barrett is driving the elementary school bus."

I looked back to Jeb and I could see all these big kids sitting around him.

"Yo, Harry! You must be that famous chess player. Jeb's been telling us about you," I heard someone yell.

"Harry, back here," Jeb was waving frantically.

It was great to see Jeb again and to catch up. We only made two more stops after mine and then headed out of the city. Jeb and I spent almost the whole bus ride talking about our summers. We dropped the high school kids off first and then went on to the middle school. As we pulled up to the back entrance, Jeb told me that he would be my personal tour guide. The way he said it made me laugh.

As we got off the bus, our new principal, Mrs. Goodfield, welcomed us. She introduced us to an eighth grader named Billy, and he and Jeb brought us up to our classrooms. I was excited about being in the same room as Jack and I couldn't wait to meet Mr. Messer, our teacher.

When we got upstairs I looked for Tommy's classroom, which was right next to ours. Our bus had arrived early, so the students who lived locally were just beginning to come in. Both Jack and I had called Tommy over the last few days, but no one answered.

"No one goes out the night before school starts, so where could Tommy be?" I had thought to myself.

Mr. Messer, my new fifth-grade teacher, was standing in the doorway of our classroom greeting everybody. He was short and bald. He had these really wild, round glasses on and very tiny eyes that looked kind of lost inside his giant frames. He was so excited about seeing each one of us that I watched him for a while wondering how anyone could be that excited with each student that walked in. He really was, though. I think my Grampy would call him a "jolly" kind of guy and I know that sounds like something an old person would say, but it really fit him.

Before long, Jack arrived. Jack is sort of a low-energy kid and Mr. Messer was for sure a high-energy guy. Jack gave Mr. Messer this really odd look when he got the jolly hello and welcome to fifth grade that Mr. Messer had given everyone in our class.

After Jack entered the room, he pulled me aside and said, "Harry, do you think Mr. Messer is going to be like that all day long?"

I started to laugh because I knew it was coming the minute I saw Jack look at Mr. Messer for the very first time. Before I could answer, Mr. Messer came in and asked everyone to be seated. Then he told us a little bit about himself and promised us that this would be one of our greatest years ever. This is what he said.

"I've been teaching for almost five years and I hope to be doing it for several more years. You may not have noticed but I am quite bald. I just lost my hair early like all the men in my family. My wife says that it saves me a lot of trips to the barbershop. I love to go fly-fishing in Vermont but I only get to do that a few times a year. I play a lot of chess in my free time and I am the sponsor of the chess club here at school. I actually started it. Now how about telling me a few things about yourselves. We'll use the next half hour or so to share."

Because of where we were sitting, Jack and I got to speak at the very end. I figured Jack wouldn't say a lot, but he ended up talking about the Mercier Movers, our old chess club. After that, he told everyone about my chess tournament in Colorado. When he was done, I didn't have much left to report so I ended up talking about Zeus. Mr. Messer asked me how I got interested in chess and I told him about how my dad and Grampy taught me.

After we finished, Mr. Messer asked each of us to share one thing that we had learned about someone in the class and he made this big list on easel paper that he said he was going to hang up.

For the first time ever, I was not the only Boston student in my class. There was a girl named Tina who had been in the

Boston Public Schools and had finally been accepted to the METCO program. I had seen her on the bus in the morning and I knew she came in with me, but I didn't notice her in my class until everyone sat down.

Mr. Messer said our class was a real melting pot. We had students from France, Japan, Iceland, and Armenia. Each of them knew English as well as their own language. One student even got up and bowed and Mr. Messer bowed back, explaining that in her country this was proper behavior when you meet someone new, kind of like our shaking hands.

Once we all introduced ourselves, it was time for recess. Jack and I spent the whole recess looking for Tommy and asking some of the kids if they had seen him. We were both kind of worried, but there wasn't anything we could do. Then Jack got a great idea. We would ask Tommy's teacher if she knew why he didn't come. Just as we were about to ask her, Mr. Messer blew the whistle and it was time to go in.

At lunch, we had assigned tables. Mr. Messer had made the assignments and he said that if anyone was really unhappy with their seat they could talk to him about it. Luckily, Jack and I got to sit together. It made me sad that even if we found Tommy he couldn't even eat lunch with us. But one thing that was really cool was the food. There were tons of choices, except it was kind of expensive, and besides, I knew my mom intended to make my lunch for the rest of my school life. I did have enough money for a juice and that was awesome. Jack got one, too. After we ate we had a very short lunch recess, but still no Tommy.

Fifth grade seemed a lot like fourth grade so far. Same kind of routines but different material and this very cool homework notebook that Mr. Messer told us to never, ever lose. It even had a place in it for parents to write notes back to your teacher. Mr. Messer thought that was very hot, but none of us kids found it so great.

The day went by very fast and soon it was two-fifteen and we were packing up to go home. It had flown by because Mr. Messer made school interesting and all the stuff we did was exciting. And if it wasn't, Mr. Messer found a way to make it exciting. It was only the first day but already I liked him a lot.

When it was time to go home, he dropped a surprise on us. He said that everyone had to share at least one thing that they had learned that day in order to leave the room. Mr. Messer said that it could be about anything and some of the answers kids gave were really funny, like the fact that there are lunch aides who smile at you. One girl said that she liked that the bathrooms had big mirrors. Jack whispered that she looked like a "hair brusher." Another girl said that meeting new kids was fun. A boy said that he loved chocolate éclair ice cream bars and in the middle school you could buy one everyday. One boy said it was a relief to have a guy teacher since he was surrounded by girls at home and even his dog was a girl. Mr. Messer laughed and so did we. I shared how awesome it was to have my bus buddy, Jeb, at the same school and my best friend in my classroom. It was a fun way to end the day and it made us all want to come back.

The bus ride home was quiet. Jeb didn't have classes yet so he didn't have any new school stuff to talk about. He had just come to school to help out with the students coming to the middle school for the first time. I had seen him two or three times during the day and it was very cool to have an older student know you. It made me feel like I had an "in," if you know what I mean.

I never stopped talking all the way home. Jeb was a good listener and he had lots of nice things to say about Mr. Messer. He said that the kids really liked him a lot. I wasn't at all surprised and I couldn't wait to join the chess club.

I had a hard time keeping my eyes open. The bus was hot and stuffy and my clothes were really sweaty. I was looking forward to having an early shower. Showers are not my favorite thing, but on a hot, sticky day all I can think of is being near water.

As my bus was coming to a stop, I could see Grampy wandering up the street holding onto Zeus for dear life. I kind of had a feeling that my Grampy would find some way to be out and about when I got home. He always wanted to know about my school day. I traded my backpack for Zeus's leash and we walked around the block and then back home. While we walked I told Grampy all about Mr. Messer and how great school had been that first day.

Getting back into a school routine didn't take long. I felt rushed at night and there was not a lot of extra time to do much of anything. I couldn't even get more than fifteen minutes of chess in. I sure was glad that chess was the kind of game you could leave and then pick up again rather than one of those you had to play until the end.

After dinner, Hank stopped by to drop off a dish that my mom had left at his house, but my dad made sure it was a quick visit. You know about all those rules on school nights!

After Hank left I went on e-mail. I had a long message from Consuela asking me how the first day of school went and then I had one from Dawn giving me a heads-up on a chess tournament that was taking place in early October. At the bottom of her e-mail she talked about how excited she was to start out a school year "braceless." It made me think of Sam and wonder how he had made out at his doctor's visit. Then I started to worry a little bit about my own scoliosis. I hoped I would be as lucky as Consuela had been.

I wrote back to Dawn and told her about Mr. Messer—what he had shared with us and that he had started the chess club at our school and how I couldn't wait to join it. I also said that even though she was excited about being braceless, I was sure that no one ever really thought that she looked weird with the brace. I was hoping Dawn wouldn't take what I said the wrong way. I mean I knew she had probably felt like a "big turtle" in the brace, but Mom has explained that how you look and how you actually feel about how you look are two very different things.

After I got off my e-mail, I told my dad about the October chess tournament. He was very excited and said he would go online and see how much it cost. I hadn't been in any really big tournaments since June so I was excited about entering. I was also wondering if Dawn and I would be opponents.

When I got into bed I had trouble falling asleep because I started thinking about Tommy. How could Tommy just disap-

Chapter Twelve

pear and not tell Jack and me where he was? That just didn't happen; at least it had never happened to me before. Even my dad looked very surprised when I told him that Tommy wasn't at school and that no one had seen or heard from him. It was a big mystery.

Chapter Thirteen

Middle school wasn't really a lot different from elementary school except that there were lots of new kids bigger and older than me. Fifth grade was a lot like fourth grade except that the girls were in your face more and the boys were bigger and a lot louder.

Jack and I both joined the school chess club and we stayed after school once a week to play. It was a good way to meet other kids and also to get some good practice in before the October chess tournament. Even though I played a lot more than Jack, he had some interesting ideas and he was a good thinker, so when he made a move he put a lot of thought into it. That was really the secret to being a good chess player: stop, think, plan, and then move. Since we pretty much knew each other's game, we always tried to get different partners and Mr. Messer preferred that.

Finally, after a couple weeks of school, Tommy called. He and his mom had been out in Seattle helping his grandmother, who was very, very sick. His dad, who could work from home, moved his job out there for a while to help out. It happened very suddenly and I guess it was pretty far away to call and tell us. Tommy sounded like he was having a really hard time and was feeling uncomfortable about starting school late. I felt really bad when I had to tell him that he wasn't in the same class as Jack and me. I thought he would be really upset about it, but he said that his mom had called the school and had told him a while ago. Maybe that was why he didn't write and let us know where he was. Tommy disconnected from kids pretty easily and maybe he thought that Jack and I wouldn't include him since we were in different classes.

I tried to get Tommy out of his slump by telling him about the chess club and how cool it was. He seemed excited and we decided we would meet each day at recess and then after school at the chess club. Just as we were about to hang up, he told me that his grandmother had died. It was so strange how he just threw that in at the end of the conversation and I kind of didn't get why he didn't tell me that in the very beginning. Having a grandparent die is pretty heavy stuff. Tommy always did have a hard time with his feelings so maybe he just didn't know how to break it to me. I told him how sorry I was to hear that and then he said he had to hang up.

I wasn't sure if Tommy had called Jack and so I e-mailed Jack right away. It took me a long time to tell him everything Tommy had told me and I was hoping that Jack would take the hint and call Tommy once he got the e-mail. Jack was kind of out there sometimes with his own feelings so I was hoping that he would figure this out for himself.

My parents felt really bad about Tommy's grandmother and my dad said that I should have passed the phone over to him so that he could have talked to Tommy's mom or dad to tell them how sorry he was. That would have really freaked Tommy out. Even though I got what my dad was talking about, it was better that just I spoke to Tommy. Finally I could get to sleep at night without wondering where he was. I was really happy that he was back and I couldn't wait to see him. "Mystery solved," as my Grampy would say.

The next morning, when I got to school, I went right next door to Tommy's classroom so I could say hi and let him know how cool it was to have him back. Jack was with me, but he was still trying to understand why Tommy didn't let us know where he was. I wanted to say, "Be cool, Jack. He's back so just be cool about it," but I decided to keep my mouth shut.

Tommy's friend from third grade was standing with us so I was happy that he had already made a connection with someone in his class. His teacher seemed really nice and she came out and started talking to us, and then Mr. Messer came over. Herbie would have called it a "welcome back, Tommy, party." Anyway, we were all happy to see him again and Tommy looked very relieved to see us, too.

When Wednesday came, the day the chess club met, Jack and I convinced Tommy to join us. Mr. Messer brought Tommy over to the less-experienced-player area and found an opponent who played kind of like Tommy. Mr. Messer called it "knowledge of the game." We all had a good time and Mr. Messer even asked me to help do some coaching with the group Tommy was in. He said that it was up to me and if I wanted I could coach part of the time and play a game the rest of the time. He even asked me to be his opponent for a few matches.

It always seems like all the best activities are on the same day. That's exactly what happened with the chess club and hockey. My hockey practice with my old team, the Falcons, was on Wednesday nights, so between chess and hockey, Wednesdays were going to be "crunch days." I had to get back to Boston on the late bus, eat really quickly, and try to get my homework done before heading out to practice. I knew my parents weren't feeling good about this at all. It was really hard to have both of my favorite things on the same day and everyone seemed grouchy about it. Even Grampy asked me if my homework was done as I bounced down the stairs on my way out to practice. I was hoping my whole year wasn't gonna be like this.

Getting back on the ice with my team and Coach Miller was, as Herbie would say, "mad-good." I was a lot more nervous than I thought I would be, even though I had played all summer. I made some stupid mistakes and missed a lot of shots. I kept letting my mind play tricks on me about hitting the boards. Coach K. had warned me about how hard it would be when I was practicing at the same rink where I had gotten injured. It was our goaltender who kept covering up for me by doing a good job stopping breakaways, which is hockey talk for not letting a puck get into the goal that you didn't think was coming in the first place. We ended up coming out okay, but I didn't feel very good about my game.

The rest of the guys on the team made me feel welcome and they even played jokes on me in the locker room, the way we always used to do with each other. But I was feeling down. Just when we were about to leave, Coach Miller came in and spoke to the team.

Harry Scores a Hat Trick

"Good practice, guys," Coach Miller began. "I want each of you to remember that like all sports, hockey is a mind game and you need to have your mind in the right place to play well. Don't look back and worry about mistakes you have made in the past. Just focus on this game and start by choosing one thing that you really want to improve. The rest will fall into place. Defense needs to stay in control of the puck and I saw some good breakouts. Our goaltending was also off to a good start. You want to get that puck out and keep it out and then move in to score. This is a new season so I want everyone to look ahead and keep their minds on this year only. For you, Harry, and for anyone who has had a significant injury, this is not so easy. You will have to work especially hard to keep yourself in a good place and not look back. I know that this is going to be a strong season for everyone. See you next week. Remember, always get that homework done. We don't just want good hockey players, we want good students, too."

When he was done the guys came by and gave me five, saying how great it was to have me back. Coach Miller also came over and told me to really think about what he had said and not to be so hard on myself.

"Harry, ease up on yourself, son," said the coach. "I could see it on your face, thinking that you might hit those boards again. Pretend the boards aren't there, Harry. If this is going to work for you, you have to get yourself in the same place that you were in this summer with Coach K. He told me you played one heck of a game. It takes a lot of courage to be out on the ice. Thanks for coming back, Harry. We really need players like you. See you next week."

As I was coming out of the rink, my dad met me. He had this big smile on his face and I could tell he was ready to talk hockey.

"Harry, how was practice, son?"

Oh how I hated it when he called me son. It meant that he was warming up for a serious talk. As Herbie would say, "Big Daddy is warming up for the big talk!"

"Dad, it was a lot harder going back to the rink than I thought and I kind of want to just think about what Coach Miller said to us," I told him. "I don't feel much like talkin' about it. Right now, I just want to think about my bed, Dad."

"No problem, son. We'll be home before you know it. I had a feeling it might be a tough night for you, but I hope that you aren't being too hard on yourself."

On the way home, Dad made what Consuela always calls "silly talk," going on and on about nothing. I gave him my usual "um, um, um" for an answer. Herbie has an expression for that, too, but I won't share it.

When we got home, Grampy met us at the door and I could tell he was ready and waiting for a hockey report, too. Fortunately, my dad took over and I ran up the stairs and got ready for bed. Grampy looked a little disappointed that I didn't stop and do big hockey talk with him, but I'm sure my dad gave him a heads-up once I got upstairs. I think I was asleep before I my head even hit my pillow.

Grampy always says that life is about getting into a rhythm and keepin' that beat goin' and I was beginning to understand what he meant. I was starting to get more homework in fifth grade and it was tough going to chess club and hockey practice on the same day. I cruised through Mondays and Tuesdays but then on Wednesdays, I hit a wall. I'd kind of crawl through Thursdays and on Fridays I was half asleep on the bus on the way back to Boston. Hockey practice really wiped me out, but I realized how much I loved the game and how happy I was to be back in it.

By early November, I was pretty much into that rhythm that Grampy was talking about and I had even adjusted to my chess and hockey schedules. The tournament that Dawn and I had signed up for was very cool and they even had some of the really famous Grandmasters of chess there giving lectures and talking to people about why they made the moves and just about anything in chess that you wanted to ask them. Dawn was not shy, and she got into some very detailed questions about specific moves with them and it kind of made me laugh. Dawn did not hold back, that was for sure. Before the Grandmaster answered any of her questions, Dawn searched the crowd for me to make sure I was in listening distance of the answer.

The thing I liked most about the tournament was that Dawn and I were not paired against each other. I still felt awkward about winning the tournament out in Colorado because I knew how badly Dawn had wanted it. I mean, I think it's awesome that I won, but I still felt bad that Dawn didn't.

Hockey was going better and I was no longer thinking about the boards each time I hit the ice. I was pleased with my skating and my ability to make some aggressive passes. I also helped make some good saves and I could finally say that my head was in the right place when I was on the ice. In fact, Coach Miller was going wild at the last practice when I gave the puck such a whack that it started bouncing across the ice straight through the legs of our best goalie. I was definitely into my game.

Whenever I went to practice, I kept looking for Sam, but I never saw him and I hadn't heard from him in weeks and weeks. I e-mailed him a few times but he never wrote back. I finally asked the coach of his age group if Sam had ever joined the team. That was how I found out that Sam had had back surgery. I guess his curve was much worse than he had said and the doctors decided that he needed an operation. I felt kind of disappointed that Sam hadn't let me know since we had spent so much time together over the summer. We had even talked about his scoliosis quite a bit and it was me who stuck up for him in the locker room when someone made fun of his brace at that very first practice.

"What's this all about?" I thought to myself. "First Tommy disappears and now Sam has back surgery and doesn't even let me know. How long does it take to write an e-mail or pick up a phone?"

When I got out to the car, I told my dad about it and he was as surprised as I was. I think he knew that I was in kind of a tizzy about it, even though I didn't come right out and say that.

"You know, Harry, I was surprised about Sam not letting you know, but the more I think about Sam, I am not at all surprised," said Dad. "Sam was angry not just about having scoliosis but also about some of his family stuff, Harry, and it kind of makes sense to me that he didn't let you know. The other thing is that Sam knows that you also have scoliosis and maybe he thought he was helping you by not telling you so you wouldn't get scared about your own back."

"It doesn't really matter, Dad. I guess he just didn't think I cared or something. Maybe he never really thought of me as a good friend," I answered.

"Don't be too hard on Sam, Harry. I understand how disappointed you are, but I think there may be more to this. I think you ought to give Sam a call and see if we can make a visit to his house or to the hospital if he's still there. It's not like you to turn your back on a friend, Harry," Dad replied.

"I'll think about it, Dad. I don't really want to talk about it anymore. I'm pretty tired and I just want to think about my bed."

Chapter Fourteen

W hen the weekend finally came, I decided to give Sam a call and see how he was doing. My doctor's visit was coming up soon so I was curious to know all about Sam's surgery. I have to admit, I was freaked out by the whole idea.

Sam's mom answered the phone and when she heard it was me, I thought she was going to jump right out of her skin with excitement.

"Whoa there. It's just me, Harry Jones," I thought to myself. "Why is Sam's mama going wild on me?"

Then Sam's mom went on to explain to me that none of Sam's friends even knew about his surgery because Sam wouldn't tell them. I wasn't surprised about that at all. I think my dad was trying to tell me that Sam kind of stayed inside himself a lot.

After about five minutes of rapping about nothing special, you know, parent filler, Mrs. Stevens finally remembered that I had called to talk to Sam.

"Harry, let me get Sam so you can talk to him."

It seemed like a long time passed before I finally heard Sam's voice at the other end of the phone. He sounded really down.

"Harry. How did you find out about my surgery?" Sam asked. There was no "Hi, Harry, how are you?"

"I asked the coach of the hockey team that you were thinking of joining, Sam," I said. "How come you never called to give me a heads-up about your surgery? Hey, Sam, my man, I thought we were friends."

"Sorry, Harry. I pretty much didn't tell anybody. It was not a cool time and I was kind of nervous and a little bit angry about the surgery," Sam explained.

I felt bad that I had said anything, but I wanted Sam to know that I didn't understand why he just dropped out. After we talked for a while about his operation, I asked him if it was okay if I came and visited. At first Sam was kind of not interested in my coming, but then he said it was okay as long as it was at a time when his mom could be around. He had this lady who was with him a few days a week when his mom went to work. His sister was in high school and was not home very much so I could tell he was not digging that at all.

After I called to my mom in the background, she got on the phone with Sam's mom and we set it up to go over the next afternoon. I wasn't expecting it would be so soon, but I think Sam's mom was excited about his having some visitors. It didn't sound like a great scene over there.

We spent most of the next morning at church, had a quick lunch, and then went off to see Sam. Grampy decided to stay home with Zeus. I think he really wanted to come, but he decided that Zeus needed him, too.

Cambridge is close to Boston and it didn't take long to get across town to where Sam lived. It took the same amount of time to find a parking space. Parking was a bear, just like in Boston. My mom had baked some brownies for Sam and I decided to bring my chessboard since I knew that Sam wanted to learn how to play.

Chapter Fourteen

I thought the area of Cambridge where Sam lived was very cool. On the way to his house, we went past the ice cream store that Sam and I had gone to last summer. Sam lived upstairs in a big yellow house. Man, I had forgotten how many stairs we had to go up to get to his apartment.

Mrs. Stevens met us at the top of the stairs and looked very happy to see us. After we all said hi, she brought us in to see Sam. He was lying on his bed. He looked tired but good. As soon as he saw us, he got up slowly into a sitting position. My mom went right over and started adjusting Sam's pillow, which embarrassed me a little but that's my mom, the nurse, and I knew I couldn't change her.

"Sam, my man, you are lookin' good," I said. And he really was lookin' good, which surprised me. I never thought anyone would look so well after a big surgery. I had totally forgotten that Dawn had also looked pretty good after her scoliosis surgery, although she wasn't as comfortable as she had seemed that day.

"Thanks, Harry," Sam said. "I'm doin' great but I am *so* tired of staying inside and I am *so* bored. The stairs up to our apartment are a major problem for my back so I pretty much stay up here all the time. I'm even getting tired of everything I used to like—the TV, my video games, just hanging out. I even miss school. Can you dig that, Harry?"

Sam's mom jumped right in and started telling my parents all about Sam's surgery and her new job and how the operation went really well, but that her new job made it hard for her to take as much time off as she had hoped. She explained that she and Sam's dad took turns staying with Sam, but then they both had to go back to their jobs so they had hired this lady to stay with him. Apparently the lady's a little old but really nice and she even has grandchildren his age. Sam seemed to like her but not the sitting around part.

My mom asked a few questions about Sam's surgery. Sam seemed happy to talk about it, which really surprised me since he never wanted to talk very much about his scoliosis before. He always acted as though he thought it was really a dumb thing to have.

His mom explained that Sam had been diagnosed with juvenile idiopathic scoliosis when he was only seven. At the time, he had an X ray and the doctors told his mom that he had a lateral curve that measured about 29 degrees. I didn't know a lot about any of this, but my mom told Mrs. Stevens that this was sometimes considered a significant curve for someone so young. The doctor decided to have Sam wear a brace at night and I guess Sam was pretty unhappy about the whole deal. After a while, they got worried because Sam's curve kept getting worse and worse, so they did an MRI to see if he had anything else wrong. An MRI is this special kind of picture they can take of any part of your body and it gives the doctors a lot of information. You lie down on this table and go into this tube thing. As Sam remarked, it's like something out of his science fiction books. Mrs. Stevens explained that they did a screening MRI on Sam because his scoliosis had been diagnosed before he was ten and there was a possibility that he had something called a "developmental abnormality" at the base of his brain or in his spinal cord. Mrs. Stevens explained a little more about how they had discovered Sam's condition.

She said that Sam had gone to the pediatrician for a routine physical for summer camp and his doctor saw that his back had an abnormal curve. She told us that they followed him very carefully because he was so young. My mom was very impressed with all this. Then Sam's mom really got fired up about all the different braces Sam tried. She gave us every detail about each one. Unfortunately, his curve just kept getting worse and worse. My mother, the nurse, started talking about the Cobb angle, which is a way they have of measuring the curve. She was asking all these questions about how much the curve progressed each visit. Finally, Sam asked if the adults could go and talk somewhere else. I was getting kind of nervous, myself. Too much rapping about curves and spines and braces. I liked the way Sam was thinking when he decided to bag this scoliosis stuff and do something else.

"Great idea, Sam. I was hoping we'd get a game of chess in," I answered, happy to get away from all the hospital talk.

"Cool, Harry. I'm glad you brought your chess set. I could use another chess lesson. But first I want you to go over to my computer and see what I've been doing on it."

I walked over to Sam's computer and saw that he had been playing in a chess game. I took a look at his board; he was doing great. I had told him when we first met that, just because he had no one to play with, didn't mean he couldn't play chess.

Sam and I hung out in his room for a long time and played two good games of chess. I was impressed by how much he had learned since he had come for the overnight and played with Grampy. Just as we were finishing up the last game, Mrs. Stevens came in with ice cream and brownies. While we were eating, I decided to ask Sam a little bit more about his surgery. He told me that he was very uncomfortable after his operation and that the discomfort had lasted for about two weeks.

"Each day it got a little bit better, Harry," he explained, "but it was like nothing I had ever experienced before. I really had to listen to the doctor and not overdo it. They gave me medicine for the pain but it was kind of tough that first week or so."

I guess the nurses were cool, and Sam's mom and dad took turns staying with him in the hospital. His parents even had a kind of bed in his hospital room. He said that he was out of the hospital in five days and would have been out sooner except that he got a cold and his chest wasn't clear. He even showed me where they went into his spine. He had two incisions, one in his chest and one on his back. There were very thin lines that Sam said would get harder and harder to see once they healed.

I asked him why he had two incisions and he told me that it was because his surgeon was worried that his scoliosis might continue even after the surgery if he didn't fuse both sides of Sam's spine. He said the doctor was worried about something happening that they call a "crankshaft" and that he had forgotten the rest of it.

"Wow, Sam, too much information," I joked. "I think I get the idea."

We stayed at Sam's for most of the afternoon and started getting ready to leave at about five o'clock. We didn't really, really say good-bye until almost five-thirty. Parents are motor mouths! Each time they said good-bye they would start talking about something else. Finally, we were out the door and down the stairs to the street.

When we got home, Grampy wanted to know all about Sam. I gave him my take on things.

I decided to e-mail Dawn and tell her about Sam. Dawn was doing great and I had told her about Sam over the summer. She had also asked about him at the tournament a few weeks back, but I didn't know about his surgery then. Dawn and Consuela were the two people that I talked to the most about my scoliosis.

On the way home from Sam's, Mom told me that I had my own doctor's visit in about two weeks. So far my scoliosis seemed to be okay, but having not one but two friends with surgery made me a little nervous. Each of them had been diagnosed with scoliosis a lot sooner than I had been. I'm not sure that made a difference, but I needed something to hang on to.

Herbie dropped by just as I was finishing my e-mail to Dawn. Man did he create a ruckus when he came in. Herbie got Zeus howling and barking all at the same time, and I could hear my mom telling my dad to get things quiet so she could think about what she was cooking. This was Mom's weekend off from work so it meant serious work in the kitchen. That's probably why Herbie made his visit!

Herbie and I played with his Game Boy for a while and just hung out rapping about different stuff. Herbie always complained a lot about his classroom and his teacher. Each year it took him until about December to get adjusted and feel comfortable. At least that's what Hank said. Just when it looked like Herbie would be over for a while, the phone rang and it was his mom looking for him. I think Herbie was hoping for a dinner invitation but with the school rules in my house, no chance. Looking very disappointed, Herbie said good-bye, got Zeus riled up one last time, and left.

Dinner was my favorite—barbecued chicken, beans, and cornbread. Boy would Herbie have gone to town on it!

Chapter Fifteen

The next week of school seemed to fly by. Unfortunately, the work was really piling up. Book reports were due and we had started a research project on Native Americans. Jack and I got to be partners. Having Jack as a partner was great because he always did his share rather than piling all the work on me. Sometimes you can get a partner for a project and the partner doesn't do much of anything and you have to do all the work yourself. Teachers don't always see that and so it can be kind of annoying, if you know what I mean. I'm happy to do my share, but I am not happy about doing someone else's, too.

I liked the Read School chess club a lot and it was a good way to make connections with other kids in school. Mr. Messer was an amazing chess player and I enjoyed the times that we could play some games together. I also liked helping the other kids, kind of like when I had worked with Chetski last summer.

Hockey was getting more and more intense. Not playing for almost a year put me at a disadvantage and I could see that my team had made a lot of growth over the time I was out. Coach Miller was great and he kept my spirits up when I didn't have a very good practice. I made a lot of assists and once I even poked a rebound past our goalie, but my game wasn't steady and that frustrated me. Our first big game was coming up and I was getting nervous, but I didn't want anyone to know.

My appointment with Dr. Roberts came up on me quickly. The routine was always the same: Park in garage, get parking ticket stamped, go on up to see the doctor. At first the lady at the desk said I didn't need an X ray, but then I saw Dr. Roberts come out and speak with her. A few minutes later she came over and sent me to the X-ray department.

Once the "pictures" were done we went back to Dr. Roberts' waiting room. It always seemed like a long time before we finally got to see him.

At last it was my turn. After the X ray, Dr. Roberts' nurse came out and led us to an examining room. She asked me to take off my shoes and then weighed me and measured my height. After that, it was back into the examining room. I had to take my shirt off and put on a dressing gown with the back open. My mom told me that the gown is called a johnny. Not a Herbie or Harry!

Dr. Roberts was not an in-your-face kind of guy. He was a quiet talker and when he said anything to you, you knew it was important. He turned on the X-ray machine light, which was up on the examining room wall, and put up my new set of pictures. As he was placing them, he apologized for having me X rayed and said that it would not be happening each visit. He just needed something with which to compare my first X rays. My mom sat quietly, waiting to hear what Dr. Roberts learned from the new set. After a few minutes he put up the first set of X rays that he had done about six months before. As he put them up, he started asking me if I had gone back to hockey. I thought it was very cool that he remembered I even played, but then again that's kind of how they found my scoliosis. I had that hockey injury from hitting the boards and when they did the X rays and MRI for my injury, they told my parents that it looked like I had a possible scoliosis. What a bummer that was. Kind of like a double whammy!

I told Dr. Roberts about how I was back playing hockey and that I was now a fifth grader in the middle school. He told me that he also had a son about my age. I liked Dr. Roberts and I was getting to know him better, so having the appointment was not such a big deal anymore.

"Harry, let's take a look at your back, now. I'd like you to slip off your jeans, keep the johnny on, and walk across the room for me."

After I did that, Dr. Roberts asked me to bend over, almost in a dive position, and I could feel his eyes looking up and down my spine. Then he asked me to get up on the examining table so he could check out my legs. I was thinking, "Whoa man, my legs? Hey, I'm back in hockey, leave my legs and my feet out of this!"

"Harry, I know you're probably wondering why I'm checking out your legs," said Dr. Roberts. "Well, I need to see if they're the same length and if there is any involvement with your hips. I'm not necessarily expecting to find anything, but I do need to give you a thorough exam."

While he was checking me out, he asked if I was still a big basketball fan. At my last appointment he and I had talked about the Celtics, our Boston basketball team. I was blown away when he remembered that. I explained to Dr. Roberts that I was so busy with hockey that I hadn't really kept up with the Celtics. Besides, the season had just started. Just as I finished my sentence my mom gave Dr. Roberts the goods on my chess and how I had won the big tournament in Colorado. Man was she ever fired up. I could tell that Dr. Roberts was waiting to tell us about my back, but first he let Mom finish up with the chess.

"Well, Harry, it appears that you have lots of good things going on in your life and your back can join that list," said Dr. Roberts. "Your X ray indicates that there is almost no change in your curve. It is holding at about 20 degrees, which is what it was at our last visit. You've had an impressive growth spurt and you appear to be almost two inches taller than you were six months ago. The fact that your curve has not really progressed is a good sign. I'd like to see you again in about six months just to be sure things are holding well, but I am remaining optimistic. If there is any progression then, I might suggest an exercise program, which is something that is beginning to be explored for scoliosis patients. Things seem to be going well so for now I would just enjoy your school year and being back at hockey."

"Mrs. Jones, do you have any questions?" asked Dr. Roberts.

"No. I'm just happy that Harry's curve seems to be stable," said Mom. "Recently, he's had two friends who have had surgery so I'm sure he was nervous about his visit today."

"Well, Harry, just remember, you don't often hear about all the patients with scoliosis who don't need surgery, so think positive Harry."

My mom and I both thanked Dr. Roberts and I was feeling much better after getting such a good report.

Once we got on the road, the traffic was not as heavy as it usually is when we have to go across town at the end of the day. Either that or maybe Mom was just getting better at getting us in and out of it. We were home by six o'clock and that meant I had time to call Jack and find out if I had missed anything special at school. My mom had picked me up early so that I could go to the doctor so I missed reading and science. The homework was just an excuse to call Jack. I really wanted to let him know how great my doctor's appointment had gone.

Jack, who never really liked doctor talk, was very excited for me and said that he just had a feeling that I was going to get lucky this time. That really surprised me since I didn't think Jack even thought much about stuff like this. He even told me that I had looked kind of worried at school. He mentioned that Tommy had also said that I was not myself. I guess I was more worried than I had imagined. The good news is that I got good news!

Since it was a long distance call to Jack, I didn't stay on the phone very long. We decided that if I had time we would e-mail each other after dinner. Besides, I wanted to get a head start on my homework so I could challenge Grampy to a game of chess.

I zipped through dinner. While my mom went into all the details of the doctor's appointment, Grampy and I went off and set up the chessboard.

I could tell by the way Grampy was playing that my mom had told him it had to be a short round. Grampy was not that focused and early in the game I got a big advantage. Before long I had taken his Queen and Rook. His King had absolutely no escape so it was checkmate for me and very sad for Grampy. I went off to bed feeling that my day had been pretty awesome.

Having my doctor's appointment behind me was a much bigger deal than I had thought. I enjoyed middle school and was getting more and more into hockey again. Chess continued to go well and I was looked up to as a chess champion by many students, even those older than me, which was really hot! I was in a much better place than I had ever been before and I was feelin' good! Mr. Messer was an awesome teacher and he made school exciting, and when it was hard, he was always willing to help you out. Having Jack in the classroom made it even better, but I was also connecting with new kids who had not been in my elementary school. The good part was that there were also more Boston students in the Read Middle School and Jeb was one of them. In every way, I was feelin' good, and I think Jack and Tommy were feelin' good, too.

Tommy took up skateboarding with a few of the kids in his class and it was not unusual for him to bring his board into Boston when he came to visit. Even though Jack was not very hot on skateboarding, Tommy was so awesome that Jack was coming around and seeing it as a skill and not something stupid. A little after school started, Jack decided to go back to soccer. He was really nervous, but once he got to the first practice he was very cool with it. I went to two of Jack's games and I spent as much time watching how the coach handled the kids as I did seeing Jack play. My Grampy says that coaches and teachers make a big difference in kids' lives. Now I know what Grampy means.

My schedule was busy, busy, busy, and once my weekend hockey game was over, I felt like I had run a marathon. There wasn't any extra time and if I added a chess match, I was asleep before I even hit my bed. I was even too tired to hang out with my friends, but I loved what I was doing. A few times my dad helped me out and convinced my mom to let me sleep in on a Sunday and pass on church. My mom was not a supporter of missing church so it was something big when I was allowed to do that.

Thanksgiving was coming and I couldn't wait for Consuela to visit. She was bringing her new boyfriend, Stan, who sounded very, very cool. He played basketball at her college so my dad was trying to hook us up with some Celtics tickets.

In preparation for the holiday, Mom was cleaning like a wild woman. My dad and Grampy joked about her getting home from work, even if it was midnight, and finding something to clean before she went to sleep. This was all because Consuela's boyfriend was coming. I was sure glad that she kept her cleaning out of my room.

Chapter Sixteen

Having Consuela and Stan home for Thanksgiving was awesome. Stan wanted to be a sports announcer and he had this deep, deep voice; everything he said sounded important. Herbie and Hank came over to meet him and even one of Herbie's brothers dropped by for a few minutes.

On Saturday, Consuela and Mom went out to do errands and I showed Stan the neighborhood. Dad met up with us for lunch and we went to Bob the Chef's on Columbus Avenue, which is an awesome restaurant with the most delicious chicken I have ever tasted (don't tell my mom).

Since my dad was only able to get three tickets to the Celtics game, he gave them to Consuela, Stan, and me. At first I felt bad that my dad was gonna miss the game, but he promised that he would get to go to another one later in the season.

One awesome thing about living in Boston is the public transportation system. You really don't need a car to get around unless you decide you like driving. Parking is really expensive, so we have always used "the T" and it usually gets us where we need to go.

When we got to the game it was jam-packed. Thanksgiving weekend was a big time. We weren't ready to eat so we went in, found our seats, and got settled. Stan asked if he could wander around and check out the FleetCenter, which is the place where the Celtics and the Bruins now play their home games. I heard him asking one of the guards for directions to the announcer's booth or whatever you call it. It gave Consuela and me some time alone.

Consuela always wanted to know how school was going since she had also been part of the METCO program but had gone to school closer to Boston. I told her all about Mr. Messer and how awesome the chess club was and how cool it was to have Jack in my class again and Tommy right next door. Then we talked about hockey and I told Consuela how great it felt to be back on the ice, but also how every once in a while I still worried about the boards. Even though Stan was very cool, I was kind of sorry when he came back since I liked having Consuela to myself.

"Man, this is one huge place," Stan whispered under his breath. Consuela answered before I even opened my mouth.

"Well, Stan, you should have seen the old Boston Garden. It wasn't as big but it was such a cool place and it was sad for all the Boston fans when they tore it down. My Grampy says it was one of the saddest moments of his life. But, you're right. This is one huge place. Harry and I think it's great but we didn't spend years and years in the old Boston Garden like our parents and our Grampy."

"I hear ya," was all Stan said when Consuela finished. People who don't live in Boston don't always get it, but I knew what she meant.

The Celtics were playing the New York Knicks and it was one exciting game. They went into overtime and the last five minutes of the game were wild. People were yelling and screaming like crazy. The Knicks won in the end but it was very close; they won by only one point.

As Stan said, "That's all it takes, one more point and you can be the winner."

When the game was over and we went outside, the quiet almost hurt my ears. Stan asked if we could walk a bit so he could get a feel for the area. It was a cool night, clear as could be, and I could see my breath each time I spoke. I loved the beginning of winter and this was the kind of night that reminded me that winter was on its way.

Once we got into the downtown area, we hopped on the subway and were home within ten minutes. There was almost no one on the train and it was so different from during the day, when each car was packed like a sardine can.

When we got home, I was surprised to find everyone in bed. Consuela and Stan decided to walk Zeus. I said good night and went off. It had been a great night and a great weekend and I was sad that Consuela and Stan would be leaving in the morning.

Chapter Sixteen

On Sunday Sam called to see if he and his dad could come to one of my hockey games. He said he was doing much better and that he was back in school and even carrying a few books. His parents were very pleased with how his surgery came out and I guess they thought his back looked a lot better. He seemed happier and not angry like before.

Going back to school after Thanksgiving break was easy because in less than a month we had more time off for Christmas. That also meant that Consuela would be home for almost three weeks. The work was getting harder and harder at school and we had another project due in less than two weeks. I liked the way Mr. Messer broke down our projects. For each section, there was a mini-deadline rather than one big deadline for the whole thing. Most of the time, Jack was my partner, but for this project we had to work alone and it made it a little easier since I could do it on my own time without worrying about getting back out to Jack's or Jack getting into Boston to finish it. The hardest part about traveling so far to school was that when you wanted to work on a project you were often miles away from one of your partners. Some of the Boston students had trouble finding a partner who would come to Boston to work with them rather than the Boston students always having to go in their direction. It could get tricky.

Once our projects were done we were only days away from starting our holiday vacation week. Mr. Messer said since everyone did not celebrate Christmas it should not be referred to as a Christmas break. I had never really thought about that before, but he was right. Lots of my schoolmates didn't celebrate Christmas. Mr. Messer was very much into celebrating people's different customs and backgrounds and you could tell by the bulletin boards in our room.

It was strange not having a sing-along the last day of school before our holiday break, like we did at Mercier. I finally realized that I would never be back in elementary school again and it made me want to go back to Mercier and visit Mrs. Lamont and Mrs. Starck. I thought about them all the way home on the bus that last day.

Work was really busy for my mom so the house was a little crazy as we were trying to get everything done by Christmas. My mom did a lot of cooking and baking, and my Grampy said that it seemed like all of Boston was getting a taste of her kitchen. My mom never bought a lot of Christmas presents. Instead, she baked for people, and each year they looked forward to getting her special gifts.

Christmas was on a Monday so there was not a lot of time to get ready. I even had a Saturday hockey game. That meant my dad would be with me and not at home helping my mom. Consuela saved the day by coming in that afternoon and helping out. The kitchen was off-limits and there was flour everywhere, and I don't mean the kind that you see in a garden. I mean the white powdery stuff that gets on your hands, your clothes, the floor, everywhere. Even Zeus was starting to look like he had white fur and not black!

Christmas was great, even the three hours we spent in church. There was lots of singing and celebrating and visiting with family and friends. Many of Consuela's friends stopped by to visit. Our house seemed the way it used to be when she was living at home. Zeus howled each time the doorbell rang and then my mom or dad would run around trying to hold onto him so he wouldn't get loose. Grampy would call out, "Don't let Zeus get loose, don't let Zeus get loose!"

During the holiday break, Sam came to watch my hockey game. It turned out to be a great one. The winning point was scored at the end when the puck went right through the defenseman's legs into the goal. The crowd went wild and the noise level in the rink was amazing. When the game was over, Coach Miller told us that the Falcons were in a good position compared to others in the league. We were scoring goals in more than one period of the game. Coach Miller said that some of the other teams were in a real slump and had remained winless through most of the early part of the season. Nothing seemed to snap them out of it and it was definitely to our advantage. I was feeling good that my pacing had improved. Finally, my injury was behind me and all I worried about was where the puck was and who was on my side.

Chapter Sixteen

After the game, I came out and invited Sam to come into the locker room and meet some of the guys. I introduced him to Coach Miller, who had talked to Sam's dad at the end of the summer about helping Sam to connect with a team. Unfortunately, the surgery happened and so hockey was not in the picture. What I didn't realize until Sam started to chat with Coach Miller was that the doctors did not want Sam to go back to hockey ever again because it is considered a collision sport. I felt really bad when Sam explained this to Coach Miller and I wondered why he hadn't told me this when I had gone over to visit him.

On the way out of the locker room I asked Sam how long he had known that he wouldn't be able to play hockey again.

"Harry, that's why I was so angry about my scoliosis," Sam said. "The doctor was very honest with me from the beginning and I knew if I had the surgery, I'd be looking at basketball instead of hockey. Hockey is the only sport I had ever played or even wanted to play. My dad played hockey so it was kind of in my genes and it was something that my dad and I had spent a lot of time doing together. It's been really hard but I've gotten a little help with working this out and hopefully basketball will take the place of hockey."

"Sam, basketball is one of my favorite sports," I said. "My dad and I try to go to at least one Celtics game each year. And you know my Boston friends and I play basketball in the park next to my house. But I think I kind of know how you're feeling. When I injured myself in hockey last year and they said I couldn't play for the rest of the season, I had a rough time. But then I started playing chess a lot. I know this sounds odd, but after a while, even though I still missed hockey, I was so into chess that it was okay not playing hockey."

"I know, Harry, but the difference is that you knew you could go back to hockey. For me, this is it," said Sam.

" I know that it's different for you, Sam, but I am hoping that it will work out the way chess worked out for me."

I could see our dads waiting, so Sam and I wrapped up our hockey talk. I was starting to understand a lot more now that Sam told me the whole story. For a long time I thought he had real attitude, but now I finally knew where it was coming from.

Our holiday break ended a lot sooner than I wanted and before I knew it, we were taking down the Christmas tree and I was getting back into my school routine. My mom and dad were like trained robots. There was no staying up late the night before school was to start.

Consuela's break was much longer than mine so she spent part of her time working in one of the Boston department stores earning some extra money. Then she decided to head back down to Atlanta a little early so she could have a visit with Stan's family. I was wishing that Stan could come back up to visit us instead, but I knew that it was too expensive. Besides, Mom said that Consuela really liked being in Atlanta because she got to do what she wanted. It would be a long time before I would get that chance.

Chapter Seventeen

We had an awesome snowstorm the day school was to start again so my holiday break lasted an extra day. I spent almost the whole time hanging out with Herbie and Hank and watching movies. Mom stayed at the hospital and worked into the next shift until the other nurses could get in. Dad worked at home, something he only did during emergencies, but two feet of snow was definitely an emergency. The next day school was cancelled again, at least for the town my school was in. Boston had a delayed opening, but that didn't help me out since Herbie and Hank had to go in. I ended up playing chess with Grampy for most of the morning and then I took Zeus out for a long walk. It was too slippery for Grampy to be out. The snow had melted and then froze to ice during the night, not great for walking.

Right after I came in from my walk, the phone rang and it was Jack. He sounded even more bored than I was. We decided to play a chess game online. My dad had taught me how to set it up and this was the very first time I played with Jack on the computer. What was weird was not hearing all his groans and sighs as we played. It took some getting used to, just sitting there in complete silence looking at a chessboard that someone, whom you couldn't see, was making moves on.

Jack and I played almost three games and then my mom called me to do some chores. I was ready to quit at that point, anyway. I was distracted because I was already worried about another snow day. I wanted to get out and see my friends at school and get back into a routine. Vacations are nice, but man, I needed a little more to do.

The next morning I was up even before my alarm went off. I was so happy when the man on the radio did not announce "no school" in Boston and the town where my school was which meant the Boston bus would be ready to take me to school.

I got to my bus stop so early that I ended up waiting almost ten minutes before the bus finally came. As soon as I got on, all the bus kids high-fived me and I could see Jeb way in the back, with the usual big grin on his face. He and I spent the whole bus ride going over all the stuff we did on vacation. Basketball was his big thing and for Christmas he had gotten tickets to the Boston Celtics/Houston Rockets game. Jeb got so into it that I felt like I was watching the game, not just listening to someone explain it. At one point he stood up on the bus to show how one of the baskets fell and Bob, the bus driver, told him to sit down.

Just as we were pulling up to school, Jeb asked me about hockey. I told him that we had had only one game during vacation and that our team was really hot this year. Even though Jeb was not at all into hockey, I liked that he cared enough to ask me about it. Besides, I had unloaded a lot of Sam's stuff on Jeb and I knew he would be happy to know that Sam had come to one of my games. I wanted to tell him more about Sam but there wasn't enough time.

Getting back into school was better than I thought it would be. Tommy met Jack and me in the hall as he was going into his room and was all fired up. He had gone back out west to close up his grandmother's house and I guess he decided that it was not so bad out there in Seattle. I remember how beautiful it was out in Colorado last June at the chess tournament. Tommy was right; it was a whole different scene.

Just as we were getting into all the good stuff about Tommy's trip, the bell rang and Mr. Messer came out and gave us the high sign to go into the classroom. Mr. Messer was very happy about being back and he got all of us just as excited. During math, he showed us a PowerPoint presentation of the kitchen he was remodeling, which was a lot of fun. At first we thought he had gone over the edge, but then as he moved into all the angles and the measuring, we got the picture of what he was trying to do. He was using a real-life situation to help us connect to math and it worked. Then Mr. Messer had us all drawing plans of our dream kitchens, but we had to end up with a specific measurement when we finished. I never thought of anything but cooking and eating in a kitchen and doing a lot of rapping. This was a whole new way to think about a kitchen and it was an awesome road back into math.

The day was broken up into mini-projects to settle us back into our schoolwork. Mr. Messer always said that learning was about making connections to real life and I was beginning to see what he was talking about. Even though he was very different from Mrs. Lamont, they were also a lot alike. They both made learning fun and talked about things in their own lives that kind of hooked us in. Each of them wanted feedback and gave us chances to tell our own stories, which helped us to get to know each other. Best of all, neither of them ever lost it with anyone in the class. Jack said that some of the kids who had Mr. Messer before called him "Steady Eddie" because he is such a great teacher. He also told me not to share that with anyone, so whatever you do, don't say I told you.

The bus ride went by really quickly and soon it was time for Jeb to get off the bus, and then my turn. The ride home had gone by so-o-o-o fast, even though the roads were not that great.

I had a lot of homework so I decided to get right to it. I didn't always do that, but I was really fired up about school and I wanted to get some of my work done before my dad got home. I had taken out a new book from the school library and I was anxious to start reading it. I was into mystery stories and this one had just gotten some kind of award. I told Jeb about it on the bus and he said it was an awesome story. Since I am a "read each word" kind of person, it takes me time to get into a book. I always wanted to be a faster reader, but Mr. Messer says it's more important to understand what you read.

The next morning was so sunny that the snow made the ground look as if it were covered with shiny, clear crystals. The sidewalk was still a little icy so I had to be careful walking to the bus. By lunch recess, a lot of the snow had melted and everything was dripping with water. At recess we all just hung around the blacktop and talked. After school I went to chess club. It felt good to be back and we had some new kids on both levels. One of them had been in Mrs. Lamont's class last year and he said he had decided to try chess because I made it sound so exciting. He made me feel really good when he told me that. He had played soccer in the fall so he hadn't been able to start earlier. I ended up spending most of my time teaching him the game.

After school I raced through my chores and homework and by the time I got to hockey practice, I was dead tired. Coach Miller was really excited because one of the other teams that had been a little ahead of us was now trailing by two games. That meant we might have a chance at the playoffs in March if we could continue with our winning streak. I went from feeling dead tired to being full of energy and couldn't wait to strap on my skates and get out on the ice. My dad brought the newspaper with him and sat and watched my whole practice. I think he was as excited as Coach Miller about the possibility of the Falcons making the playoffs. He even let out a whistle when Coach Miller gave us the news. Go figure. That wasn't like my dad at all. I think my Grampy was rubbing off on him.

The team was really hot on the ice and we had a great practice. Coach Miller had divided us up into two teams. My team had a lot of assists and finally scored a breakaway goal that gave us the game. It felt really good to be on the winning side. There was more checking now and it was often between the player and the boards and that didn't even bother me anymore. I kept my focus and was playing more consistently.

January seemed to fly by. In the middle of the month we had a long weekend in celebration of Dr. Martin Luther King's birthday. That Friday we had an assembly at school and a group of African-American dancers put on an awesome performance, teaching us some early history and what each dance meant. Then they taught us some songs and the program ended with all of us trying one of the dances. That same weekend my church had a special time during the service to remember Dr. King and other great African-American role models. At the end, any member of the congregation could speak about role models in their own lives. Grampy never came to church with us because he said it took too long, but on this one morning my mom would not let him stay home. Finally he agreed to go and when they asked people to share stories about their own role models, my mom got up and spoke about my Grampy. That made me so proud. She got a little gushy, but Mom was right. Grampy had no special school degree, but he was a great teacher and he taught everyone to always "stand tall and be proud of who you are."

On Monday, a holiday, we drove out to school for a special breakfast to celebrate the life of Dr. King with the community where my school was located. Mr. Messer was there so he got to meet my Grampy. Once Grampy got Mr. Messer cornered, I think he was the last person Mr. Messer got to talk to, but he and Grampy looked like they were having a good time. Jack and Tommy and their families were also there. It was a chance for some of my new friends to meet my family and for me to meet theirs. It ended up being a much longer event than had been planned, but everyone had a great time. I kind of wish I had met Dr. King since there was so much fussing about him. He must have been someone really, really special.

By early February we had missed two more days of school and there was snow everywhere. I was getting tired of shoveling and walking Zeus on slippery sidewalks since he took off after everything he saw. Jack's family had decided to take up cross-country skiing and Sam was still thinking about basketball. On one of the snow days, I ended up playing chess with Dawn on the Internet for most of the day. She was on a tournament-winning streak. I had passed on some of the tournaments because of my hockey schedule, but I signed up for one over February vacation along with Dawn. She was like my chess point person and I didn't even have to look at the calendar of chess events anymore because Dawn would tell me. I also got a lot of stuff in the mail now because of the Kings of K–12 Tournament. At this point I was pretty much a "chess guru," at least that's what Tommy called me.

Mrs. Starck, the Mercier principal, asked Tommy, Jack, and me to school to talk to the students about chess at one of her assemblies. It felt great to be back at our old school and to see all of our teachers. The assembly was at the end of the day and afterward we spent the afternoon helping out at our old Mercier Movers Chess Club. While Jack and I coached, Tommy got right into a game. His opponent was a third grader who was awesome at chess and she ended up coaching Tommy. This girl did not hold back, even though Tommy was two years older. At the end Tommy looked shocked that she had won so quickly. It made Jack and me smile seeing Tommy's reaction.

Life was treating me real good and I didn't even think about my scoliosis anymore. In school, I noticed there were a few kids in back braces and I think they probably had scoliosis but I never asked. I finally gave in and started the exercise program from Dr. Roberts. The exercises kept me in good shape for hockey and mom let me watch TV while I did them. They only took about forty-five minutes and I hoped they were helping my posture. Even though it was hard getting started, I always felt good when I finished. My mom said that some doctors didn't think the exercises really help, but nobody really seemed to know for sure. They can't take the place of surgery, but my scoliosis was very mild and the exercises were helping me to stand up straighter. Dawn said that she still did some back exercises, so I think they must help. Dawn wouldn't do anything if it's just stupid stuff.

In science we were studying the human body and the spine and I was learning more and more about what happens when someone has scoliosis. Last year I couldn't even say the word "scoliosis." In class, we learned that there are a lot of medical conditions that have a big effect on your life but, because they are not life-threatening, people don't talk about them a lot. Scoliosis is one of them and it can get a lot worse than people realize. Mr. Messer said that it is really important for us to know about all these things since many students have some of these conditions and as a school family it is important that we understand.

By February vacation, the Falcons were hotter than ever with a winning season and no injuries. I had played in a weekend chess tournament with Dawn and came out a winner, which allowed me to participate in another big tournament in June if I was interested. Chetski had taught me some of the openings that I used and I think Dawn was really surprised at one of them. I was glad that I had not given up chess when I went back to hockey. At times, it was difficult because I had to organize my time so that I got all my homework done and then still had time for my chess and hockey schedules.

By early March, it was getting harder and harder to concentrate in school. While the rest of my class was thinking about how exciting our April ecology camp trip was going to be, all I could think about was the Bantam Hockey Invitational State Tournament. I think my mom had given Mr. Messer a heads-up about it because each Monday he would ask me how my hockey team did over the weekend and Mr. Messer was definitely not into contact sports. Having been out of hockey for a whole season because of my injury, I found this awesome. Even Dawn, who used to say "hockey, smockey," was getting into it and her e-mails always asked for a team update. Sam was the most excited and I think it was his way of still being part of a sport he really loved but had to give up. Even Stan was involved and he put hockey notes at the bottom of Consuela's e-mail asking me all about the team. Mom was beginning to show signs of being a true "hockey mom" and was much more involved in what the team was doing. As soon as she started to show any excitement, she would catch herself and give me this long, long talk about school and chess and hockey and keeping myself centered. The only center I was thinking about was the teammate who would be playing center forward on our hockey team, but I didn't tell Mom that. It was better to let her think I was taking it all in.

When the day finally came for us to play the deciding game in the district elimination process, I was feeling very, very nervous. We were playing at a rink in Milton, a nearby town, and it seemed like the whole world was going to the game. Part of me was not at all sure that I wanted them there. The pressure was big and my teammates and I were feeling it. In the locker room before the game, Coach Miller helped us all work through some of that stress, but some of it was just going to be there no matter what he said to us. In a way, I felt as if I had been in the same place once before, that day out in Colorado when Dawn and I were opponents at the Kings of K–12 Chess Tournament. What was different about this pressure was that an injury had brought me to chess and this time I was trying to avoid an injury and still play hard.

I knew a lot of the guys on the other team and I also knew that they needed this win as much as we did. Some of their players were huge compared to us, but Coach Miller said not to let that bother us. We had kind of coasted through this season and really found a hot streak and stayed with it. Coach Miller kept telling us before every game, "Dream big and you'll get there." He reminded us that no matter how good your season is, the final measurement is how well a team does in the playoffs.

The game started out slow, with a lot of noise coming from the bleachers, which always took me a while to block out. Our opposition, the Bears, had just slipped into this game because of injuries on other teams, which had allowed them to win two big games and qualify. Their season had started out very slowly so they were really fired up for a win. I sat on the bench for the first five minutes of the first period. The matches between the forwards and the defensemen were strong. Coach Miller called a time-out and put me in. He told us to keep our feet moving and get the puck in as deep as we could. Just as the second period ended, one of their players tried tripping one of ours with a stick and got a trip penalty. He was one of their better players so their coach was not happy at all.

When it was time to begin the third period, we had our orders from Coach Miller. He sent me back in and told me to pick my spots and keep it simple. I had already had several assists, but no goals. The Bears had started to put the pressure on. Suddenly I saw an opening and slipped the puck between two of the Bears. One of our forwards gave it a slam and into the net it went. The bleachers went crazy and people started to blow horns and whistle so loud that someone had to quiet them. Early on in the third period the score was Falcons 1, Bears 0. The Bears had gotten more penalties and their coach was looking pretty defeated. He just sat there shaking his head. I felt kind of bad for the team, even though I wasn't supposed to be thinking of them.

By the middle of the period we knew we were on a roll, but Coach Miller warned us not to feel too sure until the final buzzer sounded. We had done some great passing. There was a lot of body checking during the last five minutes of the period. The Bears were getting desperate. We knew if we won this game, we were on our way to the tournament for the state title. The last two minutes of the game Coach Miller put in one of our newer players and everyone thought the coach had really lost it. But Alvaro surprised us all. He definitely was playing to win and made three assists within his first two minutes on the ice. Suddenly he saw an opening and whacked that puck around the side and into the net. With only ten seconds left, we knew we had won the game and the cheers that were coming from the bleachers were like nothing I had ever heard before. The buzzer sounded and Alvaro was up on the shoulders of two of our biggest players, with the rest of the team around cheering. Our next stop was the tournament and a chance to go for the state title.

Chapter Eighteen

The next few days I was on such a high that I don't even remember what I did except talk about hockey. Mom danced around the house, and Dad and Grampy talked about hockey nonstop. Mr. Messer had made a big sign on the blackboard congratulating my team. That was awesome since my team was from Boston and most of my classmates played on a team out where my school was. They had not made it to the state invitational. I think Tommy was more excited than I was, and Jack, who really didn't like hockey, was following all the other Bantam teams online. Only Jack would think of that.

School was really busy and we were getting ready for our ecology trip to Cape Cod. I had learned that the hockey tournament would start the last day of ecology camp so I would be missing part of the camp to attend my last hockey practice. I was really bummed out that it all had to come at once. Mr. Messer was great about it and said that I could go to camp on Monday, Tuesday, and Wednesday. Unfortunately, I would be missing the talent show at the end and the round-up activities. The tournament was also on the Cape, but first I had to go home for a practice so it was very confusing.

Chess club was great and most of the players were doing well and enjoying chess a lot. The ones who weren't doing so great were moving their pieces too quickly and not thinking about the move first. A few of them were in my class and that's kind of how they worked in class, too. Mr. Messer said that the most important thing was that they had a good time and I think they were enjoying it.

The most exciting part of my week was hockey practice and we only had a few more before the big tournament. Coach Miller worked hard to get us down from our "winning high" to focus on what was ahead and that was not easy since we were all very excited. We had played well against the Bears but we had also made some mistakes, and his job was to help us to play even better in the tournament.

Mom spent the next two weeks getting all my stuff ready for ecology camp. She ironed labels on just about everything I owned, and on the stuff that she couldn't iron a label on, she used magic marker.

Consuela e-mailed me and said that she and Stan were going to try to come up for the tournament. A lot of my friends were going to drive down if we made it to the championship game.

In some ways it was like going back in time. Almost one year ago I was getting ready for the Kings of K–12 Chess Tournament and here I was preparing for another big event. Things never seemed to be that exciting for me when I was little and now every day was.

The night before I left for ecology camp things were nuts in my house. My mom took the day off from work and was racing around making sure all my stuff was packed. My dad was doing the same thing but he was in charge of the hockey equipment. My job was to check that my gear was ready for my Wednesday-night practice. Grampy, who had no job, decided that he would be our cheerleader until Mom finally told him he

Chapter Eighteen

had to take Zeus and go downstairs. He didn't look too happy about that because he always liked being where the action was.

Mom drove me out to school since I had such a big bag and she wanted to be sure I was all set. When we got there, we all had to get checked in by the nurse.

The buses were the same big coach buses that Coach Miller said we would be taking to the hockey tournament. Since not all of my teammates had cars, Coach Miller had arranged for us to have a bus. While the rest of my class was thinking ecology camp, I was sitting there thinking hockey tournament.

"Harry, what planet are you on right now? You haven't said one word to me since we left school," said Jack.

"Sorry, Jack. I was thinking about the hockey tournament."

"What made you think of that, Harry?"

"The coach bus, because we're taking one to the tournament on Friday morning."

"Harry, are you sure you can handle ecology camp because it sounds like you're already in your hockey tournament mindset?" said Jack.

"I'll be fine, Jack. I'm just getting excited about the tournament but that doesn't mean I'm not into camp. It's just odd that they both happened the same week."

The rest of the bus ride Jack and I and the other kids just joked around and talked about different things. It was fun to be away from school and to just rap about what we wanted. Still, in the back of my mind, I kept thinking about hockey.

The ride to the Cape was just a couple of hours and you could smell the ocean the closer we got. Even though we had had a lot of rain, the weather was fine and the forecast was good through Thursday.

When we got to camp, it was wild but as Jack said, "wild organized." The counselors met us at the bus and helped us take our stuff to the dorms, where we would be sleeping. Jack, Tommy, and I were sharing a room thanks to Mr. Messer and Tommy's teacher.

Lunch was a cookout and it gave us a chance to hang out and get to know our counselors and the routine of the camp. Even though the camp was very close to the water, we would not be swimming, which pleased Tommy.

After lunch they broke us up into groups with our counselors and we got a chance to explore the area. The sun was hot, but there was a lot of wind and it got kind of cold once the sun went down.

In the late afternoon we had about an hour of free time to set up our cabins and get our sleeping bags out. Tommy and I got ours done right away so we could go play hoops, but Jack seemed to be in there forever. Finally he came out and joined us but he didn't look very excited. Once we got him into a game of hoops he loosened up and seemed better.

Dinner was chicken fingers, corn, salad, rolls, and ice cream. Tommy and I were starving but I noticed that Jack ate very little. I could see that he was still off. After dinner we met as a group and got to know each other better. We also learned about our counselors, who shared a lot about themselves with us. Two of them were from Boston so for me it was a good connection. They were very cool and I could tell that we had already kind of bonded. Tommy adopted one of them and was at his side for most of camp.

When it was time for bed, I couldn't fall asleep. My mind was on fast-forward and I was playing in the first game of the championship. I'm not sure how the game went because Tommy was shaking me just when I was beginning the best part.

"Harry, wake up. Breakfast started ten minutes ago and all the showers are full. You need to get up right now!"

I raced out of bed, passed on the shower, and quickly put my clothes on. When I got to breakfast, Jack was sitting there with a big grin on his face.

"Guess you really liked that bunk," laughed Jack.

Then Tommy jumped in. "Boy, can you ever snore, Harry."

"That's cool," I answered and we all busted up laughing.

After breakfast we broke up into groups and began our day. The activities were well organized and the counselors were really involved. I found out that one of our counselors studied oceanography and had taken a year off after college to work at our camp. He said he decided to do this because he had spent his whole life in the city, but his dream was to learn and live by the ocean.

Chapter Eighteen

After dinner, we took a night walk, which I think made Tommy really nervous. He said he only liked to be places where he could see where he was going. Even with his flashlight, he could only see about three feet ahead of him so this was not at all his favorite activity. Jack and I helped him through it along with the counselor that he liked so much. I'm not sure he learned anything on the walk other than how long it took before we got back to the cabin.

Wednesday I got up early and started packing since my dad was picking me up at about three o'clock. I was disappointed that I had to leave early since I was having such a great time with Jack and Tommy. The weather was chilly and there was almost no sun, which made it a little easier to leave. The weather on Monday and Tuesday had been perfect. I knew that Jack was disappointed that I had to go, but Tommy was also a good friend to him.

My dad was right on time, and he even got a chance to meet the counselors and talk to Mr. Messer for a few minutes. I could tell that he was as excited as I was about the hockey tournament and even though he enjoyed visiting, he was anxious to get on the road because the traffic would be heavy as we got closer to Boston. The counselors were very encouraging about the tournament and wished me luck.

Practice went fine and Coach Miller spent as much time talking to us as he did coaching us on the ice. He explained how we would be seeded for the games. We would play Friday night at seven, Saturday at ten in the morning and three in the afternoon, and then the last game would be on Sunday at ten with the awards ceremony immediately following the game.

He warned us about looking ahead to Sunday and told us to focus on each game, one by one. He kept telling us not to put too much pressure on ourselves and to think before we acted about what we hoped to accomplish with each move. He ended by telling us that win or lose it was quite a feat for us to get this far. He then warned us not to think we were better than any other team and not to have an attitude.

On the way home, I told my dad what Coach Miller had said. Usually my dad had a lot to say, but this time he just listened and then told me that Coach Miller knew best.

Thursday was a free day for me since the rest of my class was at ecology camp. Grampy took care of Zeus while I slept late. I didn't realize how tired I was. Mom came in from the nightshift and went to sleep so the house was very quiet. I got up at about nine-thirty and had breakfast in front of the TV, which I was never allowed to do.

When I finished, I showered and took Zeus out for a walk. It seemed odd that none of my friends were around. They were all in school. When I got back I did my schoolwork. Mr. Messer had asked me to write up my camp experience from my camp journal and he also wanted me to do some reading.

When school got out, Herbie came over. I think he had smelled my mother's brownies all the way from school since he arrived five minutes after they came out of the oven. Hank joined us later on. Before my mom left for work, she made sure to tell Herbie how many brownies he was allowed to eat and how many he had to save for Hank. Grampy was sitting in the living room listening and called into Herbie after Mom left to be sure he had understood. After Herbie answered Grampy, he told me that he thought my house was full of detectives!

Dad came home from work later than usual. He had to stay and get a lot done since he could only work a half-day on Friday because of my tournament. He fired up the barbecue for dinner and then we went over all my hockey stuff to be sure I was all set. By the time I got into bed, I was more tired than I would have been if I had gone to school. Dad said the excitement of what was about to happen could make you tired. Maybe he was right.

Just as I was about to turn my light out, Grampy came in. He had that same look on his face that he always has when he wants to say something important.

"Harry, I know you're tired, boy, but I just wanted to say a few things to you before you leave tomorrow. I'm going to stay behind with Zeus since it's almost too much excitement for an old guy like me. I want you to know one thing. This is not about winning or losing but being proud that you got this far, Harry. In order to be a great hockey player you need to be a good friend to your teammates and never place any blame if someone makes a bad shot. Stand tall and be proud of who you are and also be proud of your teammates. Good luck."

I knew exactly what my Grampy was talking about since Coach Miller had said almost the same thing to us. The one thing he didn't say was "stand tall and be proud of who you are." That is something my Grampy has said to me my whole life and even when he's gone, I will still hear him saying it.

Chapter Nineteen

Friday was a crazy day, so much running around and getting the car packed. My mom was even more excited than I was. Zeus started howling each time we went outside and then again when we came back in. I think he knew we were all on high drive. Finally we were on our way.

When we got to the hotel, the parents acted like magnets to one another and I kind of wondered if two things weren't going on, a tournament and a parent outing. Some of my classmates from school were also there since they played on other teams and it was like one big hockey reunion.

We had an early dinner and then each team had a practice time on the ice. Ours was right before our game, which was both good and bad. We had to pace ourselves so that we weren't worn out before our game even started.

The team we were playing was very strong, with not one injury all season, just like our team. They were very powerful on defense so we had our work cut out for us. They scored five minutes into the first period, which did not help our spirits at all. The team was very slick and they maneuvered the puck like pros. They placed the shot perfectly before slamming it in. They were ahead by that one goal until the end of the third period, when we got very lucky. Alvaro checked one of their players, who lost his balance and bumped into the boards, leaving the puck wide open. With a quick assist by one of my teammates, we were tied 1–1. Neither team played well in the three periods and we each had made a lot of dumb penalties. One of our players went around the outside and caught the goalie off guard, making our second goal and giving us the lead. Finally the buzzer sounded and the Falcons had won the first game 2–1.

Consuela and Stan missed it all and arrived just as everyone was clearing out of the rink. They looked exhausted and were also starving. They had hit a huge traffic jam on the way. Most people would have been ready to turn around. Not Consuela and Stan. He was definitely the man!

My parents made me go to bed early since I had a game the next morning. I really wanted to visit with Consuela and Stan, but I knew my mom had her orders from Coach Miller. Besides, I was very tired.

The team we were playing the next morning was expected to win the whole thing so we were not looking forward to the game. They were known for their body checking and often knocked opposing players right off the puck. That made me a little nervous but I kept it to myself.

Well, I guess I wasn't the only one feeling that way since we could not seem to score one goal. By the third period they were leading 2–0 and Coach Miller looked very unhappy. He told us it had become a mind game and in our minds they had already won. He said to go out there and press and get the job done. I'd never seen him so serious about any game before.

Within ten minutes we had scored and came close to scoring again, but their goalie was fast and made an awesome save. Coach Miller kept at us and we kept at them, finally winning the game 3–2. Don't ask me how we ever managed those last two goals. I think we were all surprised. Alvaro had scored two out of three and was hotter than ever. Who ever would have thought that he could do this?

The Saturday afternoon game was not as tough. It moved much faster and we knew by the beginning of the third period that the other team was weak on defense and pretty tired. They had lost their morning game and it seemed like most of them had given up. One of their top players had broken his arm during Friday night's game so it was not a good scene for them at all. We ended up winning 1–0. We knew we had not played our best but the important thing was that we had won.

When the buzzer sounded, all of the Falcons went crazy, since winning this game meant that we might actually have a good chance of taking the state tournament. Coach Miller was all smiles and the rest of us were wild with excitement. Stan and my dad came running down off the bleachers and they were lookin' as if they wanted to join in with the rest of us.

Chapter Nineteen

When we walked through the line to shake hands with the opposing team, I felt sad and happy all at the same time. I knew how disappointed they were, and I also knew how excited I was.

There was a lot of celebrating in the locker room and Coach Miller was very psyched. He warned us not to let the win go to our heads since our next game might be against the same team we had played in the morning. They were awesome, with the best defense I had ever seen and a lot of speed. But Coach Miller didn't talk to us too long. Instead, he sent us all back to our rooms for a good night's sleep.

When I got to my room, my parents told me that Consuela and Stan had driven home to get Grampy so he could see the final game. I had really wanted him there but I didn't know my mom and dad had already thought of that.

I went in and did my back exercises. They felt really good after I had been on the ice so long, loosening me up. When it was time for me to go to sleep, my dad announced that he would be sleeping in my room with me. I wasn't sure how I felt about that but it was too late to speak up. I knew my mom was behind this. Grampy called her Nervous Nellie sometimes. How she worried about her children. It just seemed to go on forever, but Consuela said that I should feel lucky that she cares so much.

When I said good night to my dad, he was cool about everything and didn't even give me a good-luck talk. That sure surprised me. I was kind of wishing he did. I lay there in my bed for a long time. Finally, I decided to see if my dad was awake, too.

"Hey, Dad! Are you still awake?" I called out.

"I sure am, son. I haven't been able to settle down and get to sleep."

"Dad, I'm a little nervous about tomorrow's game. I think there's going to be a lot of checking and maybe some tripping, even though it's a penalty. I hope I can stay focused and not worry about an injury. When it was happening yesterday morning, I was a little distracted."

"Harry, when you play sports, it's always a mind game. You need to stay focused on playing your best and winning. You can't let your mind wander and above all you have to tell yourself that your team is as strong as the other team, if not stronger."

"I know all that, Dad, but sometimes it's hard not to think about how disappointing it will be if we lose. I mean I know someone is going to lose but I just don't want it to be us."

"Harry, think about getting some rest and stop worrying. Most of all, focus on playing the best you can and being a team player. I'll see you in the morning, son."

Both my dad and I were up early the next morning but we didn't talk much about the game. I think my dad purposely tried not to bring it up. I took a long shower and then went down to breakfast. The room was full of hockey players and they looked as tired as I was feeling. It had been a lot of hockey in a short time. Last year I was doing a lot of chess and this year I was doing a lot of hockey and some chess.

Right after we ate breakfast, we met as a team. Coach Miller told us to let our breakfast digest before we suited up and went out on the ice. I had hardly eaten and I noticed my team-mates were pretty light on the food intake themselves, but we all waited about thirty minutes and then got ready and went out. People were already in the bleachers and some were even taking photos. Flags from other state tournaments were hanging from the ceiling. About fifteen minutes before the start of the game, we all went into the locker room. Coach Miller gave us quite a pep talk, but the most important thing he said was how proud he was that we had made it this far.

"Win or lose guys, we made it to the state's, which is some-thing each one of you should be very proud of. Don't you ever forget that. Now get out there and show them who the real champs are. Good luck!"

The cheer that went up in the locker room before we filed out on the ice put a chill right up my spine.

After we filed out and they introduced the starting line-up for each team, a state policeman sang our National Anthem. I was a little embarrassed because I could feel the tears build-ing up in my eyes. I put my head down so that no one would see. As I was lowering my head, I caught my Grampy's eyes, which looked about as watery as my own.

Chapter Nineteen

When the National Anthem was over, there were lots of cheers and loud clapping and whistling and then the game began. It took about two seconds before the other team got right into checking and pressing and I could tell that Alvaro was freaking out. I hollered over to let him know he could do it. He made a solid pass to one of our forwards and the opposing team made an awesome save. This was not going to be an easy game.

By the end of the first period, we were running out of steam and the opposing team did not seem tired. I could tell that Coach Miller was worried. He called a time-out and gave us all a pep talk that got us all fired up again. By the end of the second period the opposing team had gotten a lot of penalties and things were breaking down for them. We came very close to scoring a couple of times, but no luck. The same was true of the other team. We were tied 0–0.

At the end of the second period, Coach Miller really got on us to press more and be more aggressive. He told us to toughen up and get that puck into play more. We knew what he meant but it wasn't as if we weren't trying. Maybe we weren't trying hard enough.

When we got out on the ice at the beginning of the third period, we played hard and were definitely a team on a mission. It was as if no one else were in that rink except two coaches and two teams. One of the players on the opposing side got in deep and slammed the puck with such force that it bounced off the boards and ended up right next to me. Alvaro yelled out and I whacked that puck as hard as I could. The goalie lunged forward, but it was too late. I had scored a goal. The people in the stands went nuts and before I knew it, Alvaro and my teammates were as excited as I had ever seen them. The coach of the opposing team called a time-out. Coach Miller was psyched but we all knew that there was more luck than good playing in that goal. If the puck hadn't ricocheted back toward our net, we would never have scored.

With three minutes left in the third period, the score was still in our favor, 1–0. We were all amazed that the opposing team had not scored. They had had more assists and saves than I had ever seen in any tournament. Then they came out on the ice and just kept pressing and body checking. With less than a minute left in the period, they scored. Not only did they score, they made an awesome shot. The fans were going wild. I was on the bench watching the whole play and I tell you it was something to see. It was like watching a Bruins game. Coach Miller called a time-out and told us that the game would probably go into overtime. He said that we needed to keep our heads focused on winning and not let their goal affect us. Man, what was Coach Miller thinking? We were all dragging and we were playing as hard as we ever had!

Coach Miller left me on the bench for most of the first three minutes of overtime. I was feeling frustrated because I wanted at least one last chance out there. Alvaro was also on the bench and he didn't look any too happy himself. Finally, the coach of the opposing team called a time-out.

Coach Miller looked over at Alvaro and me. "Let's see what you two have left. Get out there and play to win."

The other guys on our team looked as determined as I was feeling. I tried to get in deep with the puck but the other team was holding hard. Their goalie was amazing. He was like "King of the Saves." Suddenly, Number 2 on the opposing team changed direction and managed to steal the puck away. With a fast pass to his forward, he skated ahead and whacked that puck right dead center through the goalie's legs and into the net. With less than a minute left in the game, they had scored, taking the lead at 2–1. I saw my teammates and the look of defeat was all over their faces. It was as though something had just taken away all our energy and drive to win. When the final buzzer rang, the opposing team and their fans in the bleachers let out what seemed like one big cheer. Their mouths and bodies were moving all at the same time. They were the new state champs in the Bantam division and I don't think I had ever seen such excitement and disappointment on the ice at the same time. I looked up into the stands and my eyes met my Grampy's. I expected him to look sad. Instead, he looked disappointed but very proud.

After we shook hands with the other team, we all filed into the locker room. Some of the guys were angry and I think Alvaro was a little teary. There were so many emotions in that room. Coach Miller worked through our team, telling each one of us that we had played a great game. He gathered us all up and told us that there wasn't one thing he would have asked us to do differently. Then he told us how proud he was to be our coach and what an awesome team we were. When he said that, it kind of made my eyes water. He explained that even though it is the hope of each team that competes to come out a winner, he felt that we were all winners because of how hard we had played. He ended his talk by telling us that there are many ways to be a winner and although we were very disappointed about not being the state champs, in his eyes each one of us was a champion. For a minute I felt as though my Grampy were standing there talking to us. Grampy always says that it's not about winning, it's about doing the best that you can. Losing wasn't easy, for sure, but it was special just to be playing in the last game of the biggest Bantam tournament of the year.

Coach Miller ended by saying, "If we weren't a top team, we wouldn't have gotten this far. Be proud, not of just the game that you played, but of who you are and what you have achieved."

While we were getting into our clothes, lots of dads filed in and even with the disappointment of losing, little by little the spirit of our team seemed to improve. It was as good as it could get when you've lost such a big game. We really had played our hardest and as my dad would say, "We gave the fans a great game."

The awards ceremony came that afternoon. Some of the guys decided not to go, which Grampy said was not a good decision on the part of their families. Even though it was hard, we were a team and we needed to stay together as a team. We each received a trophy for being the semifinalists in the tournament. Coach Miller got special recognition for being a Bantam hockey league coach for more than twenty-five years, which made us all happy that we were there to cheer for him. He was an awesome coach and it made all of us proud to see that everyone agreed with us. He never got angry and made all of us feel important. No matter how good or bad our practice was, he always made us feel that we had helped the team. He didn't just care about hockey; he cared about each player.

The ride home was definitely mellow. I wanted to go with Consuela and Stan, but they had to take a different route to return to Atlanta. I was disappointed that I didn't get more time with them. Stan told me about a few tournaments that he had lost when he was my age and he made me feel a little better. It was just so hard to be on such a high note one minute and such a downer the next. My dad said that there is a very fine line between winning and losing. I guess that's what it's all about.

When I got home, I had lots of e-mails to answer but the only one I decided to reply to was Dawn's. I finally knew what she felt like when she lost the Kings of K–12 Tournament. I knew Dawn would understand how I was feeling and I kind of needed someone to know how sad I was.

At bedtime, Grampy tapped on my door. At first I really didn't want to talk but he kept tapping and I knew that he knew I was still awake. Finally, I told him to come in. I didn't feel like talking and surprisingly, Grampy knew it.

"Harry, I know this is a very disappointing time for you and there is nothing to say except to be proud of what you accomplished out there on the ice, both as a player and as a team. Remember, Harry, always stand tall and be proud of who you are. Good night and I want you to know how lucky I feel to be your Grampy."

I could hardly get the words "good night" out. I was feeling kind of choked up. As I attempted to get some sleep, I put my mind on instant replay and kept trying to win the tournament that we had just lost. Eventually, I fell asleep.

My dad drove me to school the next morning, which was great since I didn't want to face the bus crowd and go over the loss. It was a pretty quiet ride and my dad told me that if I wanted to talk about anything, he was a great listener. But I just didn't have the energy.

Just as we were pulling into the school driveway, my dad stopped the car and looked over at me.

"Harry, we need to celebrate our successes and look at our losses as an opportunity to grow. You have grown in so many ways and I hope that you remember that. Be proud, Harry."

I really needed those words to get me in the door of my school. I was dreading telling everyone what had happened.

Chapter Nineteen

I should have known that Mr. Messer made sure that the kids in my class knew first thing that morning. At first I didn't want to talk about it at all, but after he spoke to the class about the whole purpose of competing in sports, I felt much better and was kind of glad that he did that. He took time out from spelling and explained that the two most important things are being a team player and being a good friend. Then he spoke about all kinds of ways that we can feel successful about what we do on a team, even if we lose a big competition. He also said that if you don't like sports, you can find other ways to have the same experience. What he was really doing was making one of his famous mini-lessons out of my loss. Everything was a learning experience in Mr. Messer's class and even if you didn't like school, you ended up enjoying it just because of the things Mr. Messer did. He didn't just teach you school lessons, he taught you life lessons. I was lucky to have him as my teacher.

Chapter Twenty

It took about a month for me to get over losing the hockey tournament. At the hockey banquet, we all received another trophy for our season and some of the team members got individual awards. Alvaro was named the Most Improved Player and I received an award for the Most Determined. Coach Miller made it an awesome night and gave a speech that made us all proud of getting as far as we had. The parents gave him a standing ovation and the clapping went on and on until Coach Miller finally made it stop. His wife was presented with roses for her long support of hockey and for always cheering us on. As for me, I guess I finally knew that I really could do two things I loved. Chess was just as important to me as hockey and I could be a chess nerd and a hockey nerd, all at the same time.

When we got home that night and everyone finally left my room and it was time to go to sleep, I was wide-awake. I started thinking, here I was only a fifth grader and I just couldn't believe all the changes in my life. My life was like a hat trick, but instead of the usual meaning – a player making three goals in one hockey game—my hat trick was a little different. It consisted of pawns, pucks, and scoliosis, but it hadn't started out that way.

I traveled a long journey to get to a school full of strangers while my friends were back in Boston wondering why I had to go to a school way out in the country. I traveled another journey inside myself and it had taken me a long time to understand that lots of kids go to schools that are not in their neighborhoods or even convenient for them or their families. Being one of very few African-American students in a school that was pretty much White was also a journey, and at the beginning it was a hard one. People think they know, but until you live in another person's body you really don't. Sometimes there were misunderstandings, especially when the kids in the country didn't appreciate or even want to learn about the richness of my city life back in Boston. But then I met Jack and started to feel more connected to my school. With Jack there were no walls; he's just who he is and I am just who I am.

And then there was hockey. I thought my whole world would always be hockey, until my injury. Man that was so hard. I was angry. I kept ragging on myself and saying that I should have played better.

Then I started to play serious chess and I learned that you can be good at more than one thing. It was so sweet when I won that chess tournament in Colorado, but the best was that I even got to go there. Me, Harry Jones, who had never traveled at all, in Colorado.

But making friends with Dawn and knowing that my win meant her loss was a big bump for me. I remember her face when they announced that I had won the tournament.

"This is not the way it is supposed to be," I told myself.

And then there's the scoliosis that they found in my back when I got injured in hockey. I worried about that a lot, especially when I found out that kids like Dawn had to wear a brace because of it. She even had surgery on her back to make it straighter. Scoliosis sometimes runs in families and so that's why my sister, Consuela, and I both have it. What really blew me away, though, was when I started that summer hockey league and met Sam, who was in another kind of back brace. I had pretty much decided that mostly girls get the progressive kind of scoliosis, which means that the spine keeps curving, sometimes even with a brace.

But when I met Sam, I said to myself, "This is not happening. What if they put me in one of those things!"

Dr. Roberts says that there are different types of scoliosis. Each one depends on your age when you're diagnosed. Mine is juvenile, which means that it comes on between the ages of four and nine. Consuela was diagnosed during her adolescence, which my mom says could have made the tough times even tougher. But, fortunately, Consuela's case was mild. Dawn has congenital scoliosis since she had a few extra things and these extra things that were wrong with her spine actually caused her scoliosis. Dawn ended up having surgery, which Dr. Roberts says happens less and less.

Sam, the man, has what they call juvenile idiopathic scoliosis. Quite a mouthful, isn't it? That just means that it came sooner than mine but later than others, and it also started to move earlier than mine. Sam started wearing his brace when he was in first or second grade so just think how cool it was for him to stop wearing it. When he finally had the surgery, he said it was so sweet to know that he was done with braces. And also because he just wanted the whole thing over with.

My doctor says that surgery is not always the answer. He told my mom and me that new research is coming out and now some patients are not wearing braces and some are not even having surgery right away. They are trying what he calls alternative treatments. Some he likes, some he says don't work and risk no correction at all because the spine eventually becomes rigid and then it can't be fixed. Too late! Dr. Roberts is hoping that I won't need surgery because I'm very muscular and my scoliosis is sort of dormant. That means it's asleep, according to my mom. Adults can be so weird. I mean how can your spine go to sleep! I guess the important thing is that Dr. Roberts thinks that my scoliosis might be okay. I don't love the exercises he gave me, but they seem to be helping my posture since now I'm standing up straighter. They are kind of a pain to do, but I guess it's worth it if it prevents me from having surgery.

So now that you know I have gotten back into hockey and avoided the boards, I guess you think my life is pretty easy. Aren't you forgetting that I just lost a huge hockey tournament? I remember when I was little and my dad's company got sold and for almost a year he had no job to go to. Even though I was only six, I remember that those were hard times. We didn't have a lot of money and everyone was kind of grouchy for a while. There are always worries for kids. Adults need to understand that kids get anxious, too. Life has its bumps, but also its bugles to toot when things are going well.

My Grampy always talks about this really famous African-American man who used to talk to large groups. Grampy said that he talked about some journey that we go on inside ourselves. I know a journey is a trip, but I'm not sure what trip he's talking about because I don't know about everything yet. I kind of think he means the trip we have to take each time we have a disapppointment, for me my hockey injury and scoliosis. My Grampy says we will be ready for any journey as long as we feel good about who we are, even if things in our life aren't going so well all the time. Grampy says that good things can and will happen, but we have to be very patient and believe that someday we'll be able to blow our horn and celebrate. He says that if we feel good about ourselves, even the shortest person will always stand tall and be proud of who they are. My Grampy thinks that even when people are gone, part of them will always live on inside of us. Even though I am not my Grampy and I'm a lot younger than he is, I will always try to stand tall and be proud of who I am. That's the part of my Grampy that will live in me forever, I hope, and now maybe just a little of him will live in you, too. I think I'm finally ready to go to sleep. Good night.

Epilogue

Harry continued to play both chess and hockey throughout his middle school and high school years. Jack and Harry remained the best of friends, as they are today. Tommy eventually moved out west where his grandmother once lived, but still communicates with Harry and Jack by e-mail—when he remembers! Herbie and Hank are still part of the "hood" and have remained Harry's good friends. Herbie is now acting in a lot of school plays, which should not surprise you, while Hank has decided that he wants to be a psychologist when he grows up. Herbie likes to joke that someday he may have to pay Hank just to talk to him because Herbie calls a psychologist a "talk doctor." Consuela married Stan and stayed in Georgia. Harry finally has the older brother he always wanted and Stan can dote on the little brother that he always wished for. Dawn and Harry are still very close "chessmates" and each of them now writes articles for chess magazines. Harry has made many other friends in chess and continues to use the Internet to play chess with them. As for Sam, Harry lost touch with him. Sam's mom remarried and they moved around a bit, but he seems happier. The last time they spoke, Sam talked about maybe coming back to Cambridge for high school. Grampy has remained a steady part of Harry's life and has celebrated many more birthdays with Harry and his family. Zeus continues to be Grampy's faithful buddy and now that Grampy has gotten too old to walk him, Harry or his parents enjoy the responsibility. Mr. Peace died when Harry was in eighth grade and Old Blue, his dog, passed away a short time later. It seemed kind of strange for Harry not to see the two of them plodding along in the morning as he was running out the door of his house.

As for Harry's scoliosis, it has remained stable with very little progression. He goes to see his orthopedic surgeon once a year and will continue through his eighteenth birthday.

Eventually, Harry stopped doing his exercises, even though his mom encouraged him to keep on. Harry's favorite part of high school honors biology was the study of the human body, especially the spine. He knew a lot more about scoliosis after that and had a better understanding of how the spine works.

Hopefully, your life is going well and the journeys you travel are leading to many new and wonderful places, just as Harry's did. Remember that sometimes what begins as a difficult journey may open the door to something new and interesting. If it happened to Harry, it can also happen to you.

Author's Notes

W riting has always been something that I have enjoyed, but I must say that I never really thought about it seriously until 1997. I came upon it as a result of years of keeping a journal about my daughter's journey with congenital scoliosis. That journal became my first book. I have continued to write not just about scoliosis but about the different types of journeys that each of you might travel. Scoliosis is definitely a part of each of the books that I write, in addition to hockey, chess, and other topics that might interest young readers.

What exactly is scoliosis? By definition, scoliosis is a side-to-side deformity of the spine. There are three different types of scoliosis based on your age when the scoliosis is discovered: infantile (age 0–3), juvenile (age 4–9), and adolescent (age 10–maturity). Both Sam and Harry have the juvenile type since they were between the ages of four and nine when they were diagnosed. Sam's was more progressive, but fortunately for Harry, his was not. Dawn has congenital scoliosis, meaning that hers was a result of other things that were going on in her body. Dawn had three hemivertebrae, that is, one side of three of her vertebrae did not develop completely. Vertebrae are the individual bones that make up the spine. Harry and Sam have idiopathic scoliosis, which means that the specific cause of it is unknown.

It is important to remember that there are many adolescent boys, like Harry, who are able to avoid surgery because their curve does not progress. For boys like Sam and girls like Dawn who are experiencing a more progressive scoliosis, surgery is necessary to stop a very progressive curve and in Dawn's case, to do some additional repairs. In cases such as Sam's, contact sports are not recommended after surgery since there could be damage to the spine outside of the instrumented and fused area. Although the results of research studies about the effectiveness of bracing are not conclusive, most studies indicate some success at preventing the progression of curves. It is important to remember that bracing is not effective in all cases. In addition to the options of bracing and/or surgery, research is being conducted on new alternative ways of treating scoliosis. However, many of these alternative solutions have not been out long enough to indicate their long-term success. Exercise continues to be researched as an option both prior to and after surgery as well as in place of surgery. For those children who have a more progressive scoliosis, it is important that surgery be done at a time when the most correction is possible and this continues to be agreed upon by most orthopedic surgeons and spine specialists.

Who are the characters? Many of the characters' names are the names of real people who had a significant impact on my own life as a child. Harry was my grandfather's name and I think he would have enjoyed knowing that I used it for my main character. Many of my students create wonderful stories about their grandparents. A few years back I had a student who wrote amazing stories about his Poppy and that's where Grampy came from. Many of the other characters' names are those of my own friends from my years in elementary and middle school. Mr. Messer was my sixth-grade teacher some forty-five years ago and he was exactly as I described him in the book. Along with some of my other favorite teachers, he laid the groundwork for the many happy experiences I had during my years as a student. Zeus is the name of the dog that my son Colin and daughter-in-law, Katherine, adopted when Zeus was about a year old. And, finally, C.N. is Cam Neely, who played for the Boston Bruins hockey team for nearly ten years and then retired as a result of an injury. Today, Cam and his brother, Scott, put their energy into Neely House, which gives families of cancer patients a place to stay right in the same hospital where their loved ones are being treated. On January 12, 2004, the Boston Bruins will honor Cam as they retire his number alongside those of many other Bruins who gave the fans many great memories. Cam continues to be a wonderful role model to many aspiring hockey players.

Author's Notes

As each of you travels your own journey, remember that you have a variety of options which you can choose to pursue. You can play sports and still be successful at interests such as chess, just like Harry. Remember to follow your own dreams. And as Grampy would say, "Always stand tall and be proud of who you are."

About the Author

Mary Mahony has been writing about scoliosis since 1997, a result of her daughter's journey with congenital scoliosis. An elementary-school resource teacher, Mary is a strong advocate for children and feels that diversity is an important component in the ongoing development of both adults and children. Mary continues to work with children who are on a variety of journeys—educational, medical, and social. She is the mother of three who are now young adults: Breen, an architect in New York City; Colin, who has an M.B.A. and lives with his wife, Katherine, and their dog, Zeus, in Massachusetts; and Erin, who is currently in her third year of medical school in Connecticut.

Harry Scores a Hat Trick with Pawns, Pucks, and Scoliosis is the sequel to *Stand Tall, Harry*, which was published in 2002. In all of her books, Mary focuses not only on scoliosis, but on social lessons as well, and uses her characters to teach these lessons. Harry is a wonderful example of a child who is influenced by his environment, his many life experiences, and above all, his family.

About the Illustrator

Catherine M. Larkin is an art educator, illustrator, and artist whose specialty is pottery. An educator in the Belmont Public Schools, Belmont, Massachusetts, for more than twenty years, she believes there is no better job on Earth than working with kids to develop their creativity. When not teaching, Catherine enjoys creating art from reclaimed materials. She earned a bachelor of fine arts degree from the University of Massachusetts, Amherst, and a master of science in art education from the Massachusetts College of Art.